BLOOD DEBT

BLOOD AND IRON SERIES
BOOK 3

NICK EFSTATHIOU
RON RIPLEY

EDITED BY SCARE STREET

ISBN: 979-8-89476-320-0
Copyright © 2025 by ScareStreet.com

This is a work of fiction. Any resemblance to actual persons, living or dead, or actual events is purely coincidental.

ENTER THE REALM OF TERROR...

CHAPTER 1

THE WAVERLY BROTHERS

Ethan swore and picked the tooth fragment out of his knuckle. He stepped away, and Hazen chuckled.

"Told you to wear gloves, dummy," Hazen stated.

"Should've, could've, would've," Ethan grunted. "Didn't."

"No kidding." Hazen snickered. He adjusted his gloves and glanced at his brother. "How long are we supposed to do this again?"

Ethan sighed, walked to the folding table and glanced down at the notes. "Says two hours. We've got about forty-five minutes left."

"Huh. Okay." Hazen pushed on the target's forehead and peered into the man's swollen eyes. "Good. You're still in there. Think this one will take, Amir?"

Amir moaned through bloody lips but couldn't articulate anything more.

Ethan picked up a bottle of rubbing alcohol, took the cap off and dumped some of the liquid onto his split knuckles, swearing as he did so. He shook droplets of blood and alcohol off onto the wood floor and glared at Amir.

"You know," Ethan started, putting the cap back on the bottle, "this is the third time since June we've had to come to your place, Amir."

Hazen punctuated the statement with a sharp punch to Amir's ribs, causing the man to sag against the restraints binding him to the chair.

"We get paid pretty well," Ethan continued. "We'll even get a cut of what you owe. I told you that at the beginning."

"We even offered to split that cut with you," Hazen reminded Amir.

"If you'd at least pay up."

Amir mumbled in Arabic.

"Don't speak that language, remember?" Hazen asked. "Come on. Do my brother or me look like we'd go and learn whatever it is you spoke growing up? No. Of course not."

"I don't have it," Amir managed to whisper.

"Well, maybe you shouldn't have gambled, right?" Ethan asked.

Amir started to answer, and Hazen slapped him across the face, silencing him.

"Now," Hazen said, adjusting his gloves again. "Big Mike is getting kind of impatient with you. Three is usually the magic number. There's never been a fourth. So, you'll have another two weeks to get what you owe, plus the vig, to Big Mike. If you don't, that's going to be a problem."

Amir managed to lift his head and glance at them for a moment.

"Oh, I know what you're thinking," Hazen continued. "I sent my wife and kids far away. They can't be touched. Blah, blah, blah. All that good stuff. And you're right. I mean, Big Mike probably wouldn't have had them killed. You don't owe that much. But he definitely would have hurt them. Well, he would have us hurt them, and your wife is a pretty lady, Amir. There are lots of ways to hurt women. Especially pretty women. You were smart, though. You took care of them. Now, most people think, oh, my bookie's not going to kill me because he won't be able to collect if he does."

"And you're right about that, too," Ethan added.

"Except there is one thing," Hazen said. "Every so often, Big Mike needs to make an example of someone. Usually, it's someone who hasn't paid up. Someone like you, Amir, if you haven't figured out what I was getting at."

Amir's eyes widened as much as they could.

Hazen nodded.

"We don't have any orders to kill you today," Ethan stated. "We got the call, and Big Mike said to work you over for a couple of hours. Remind you what you owe. He wanted us to tell you about what's probably going to happen to you, too. You might try to run, but that wouldn't end well. He'd send someone to kill you and your entire family. They'd make it hurt, though. And you'd die last, that's for sure. They'd make you watch."

"Basically," Hazen said, picking up the story, "you're going to want to make sure you have the money in the next two weeks. In two weeks, we're going to find you, Amir. You might wait here for us. You might try to hide. I don't think you'll run, not knowing it'll cause your family to suffer even more."

"When we find you," Ethan told the man. "We're going to ask you for the money if you haven't given it over yet. If you don't have it, we're going to kill you. Kill you slow. We'll even record it."

Amir whispered in his native tongue, his body shaking in the chair.

"Not only are we going to show it," Ethan continued. "But we'll send it to your family because we will find out where they are. We'll put it up on every social media platform we can think of. It kind of guarantees that your kids will see it. Think about that for a bit. We'll also make sure people know you tried to pull a fast one on Big Mike. Anybody who comes to borrow, they're going to get to watch you die as the marker is made out."

"We want you to think about that," Hazen stated. "Think about it while you take the last bit of punishment here. And make sure you're trying to figure out a way to pay back Big Mike."

Hazen brought his fist back and smashed it into Amir's ribs.

Ethan dropped down into a chair, took out a pack of Newports, lit one, and took a long pull off the cigarette.

Beating Amir was hard work, and Ethan knew for a fact he'd be sore as hell in the morning. Not as sore as Amir would be, of course, but pretty damned sore.

"You know, he's not a bad guy," Hazen said, sliding into the passenger seat of the car.

"I know," Ethan nodded. "I like Amir. I like him a lot. Just wish he'd get his damned act together so he could pay Big Mike off."

"Big Mike likes him, too," Hazen sighed, closing his eyes.

"Oh yeah?"

"Yup. Told me yesterday when I got the assignment. Yeah, he wants the cash, but he doesn't want to kill Amir," Hazen continued. "He's got lousy luck with the horses, that's all."

"Well, he's got that gambling habit, too," Ethan reminded his brother.

Hazen chuckled. "Yeah. There's that."

"You know," Ethan mused, starting the car. "We might be going at this the wrong way."

"How's that?"

"You ever seen his wife?" Ethan asked.

"Amir's?"

"Who else?" Ethan checked the mirrors and pulled away from the curb.

"No, I haven't."

"She's built like a pro-football linebacker," Ethan stated.

Hazen glanced over at him. "For real?"

"For real. That woman's like, I don't know, six-two, maybe six-three. Easy."

Hazen grunted. "She's got almost a foot on him?"

"Yeah. Anyway, what if we told her to handle him?"

"You mean go talk to her?" Hazen asked.

"Yup."

Hazen scratched at the blonde scruff on his chin. "I guess it couldn't hurt. She's easy on the eyes, right?"

"Real easy. Her name's Asal," Ethan continued. "I bet you anything she could get him to pay up. Especially if we tell her someone might touch her kids."

"Sounds like it could work."

"She'll probably want to negotiate," Ethan added. "Think we should talk to Big Mike about it first?"

"Hell yeah," Hazen smiled. "In fact, we are out to go see him now."

"Sounds good," Ethan said. "I'm thirsty. Could do with a beer or two."

"Or three."

"No," Ethan shook his head. "Mia's got swimming tonight. I got to be straight, or Carol's going to kill me."

Hazen sighed and nodded. He wasn't a fan of his sister-in-law, but he wasn't about to rock the boat. He wanted a beer as much as his brother did. Hazen just didn't have to answer to anyone. Reaching out, he turned on the radio, hit play on the Hozier CD and closed his eyes. Hopefully, Big Mike would be good with the idea.

Hazen really didn't want to kill Amir.

CHAPTER 2
TOM DANIELS

The room smelled of lilacs and roses, antiseptics and cleansers. It was a familiar smell and one that Tom found oddly comforting at times.

"How are you, Tom?" Ava asked, bringing him a cup of coffee.

Tom smiled at her and nodded his thanks as he accepted the offered drink.

"I'm doing okay," he answered as she sat down beside him. "How are you?"

She shrugged, undid her ponytail and then put her black hair back up. "Things are a little hard here. We lost two residents yesterday and one this morning."

"All three in this wing?" he asked.

She shook her head. "One in the long term and the other two in the physical rehabilitation wing. The last two weren't expected. Your dad's doing well, though."

Tom's attention shifted from Ava's delicate features to Victor, who sat in the sunlight near one of the French doors that led out onto the veranda.

"Is he really?" Tom asked.

She laughed. "I wouldn't have said so otherwise. I don't like to tell people things that aren't true."

Tom smiled. "I appreciate that."

"Has he recognized you at all?"

"No," Tom answered. "But I'm okay with that. He gets too upset when he hears me. It's why I sit so far away from him."

There was a moment of silence, and then Ava spoke. "You know, it's not listed in his file, but I'm curious as to how he lost his sight. Was it natural? Was it an accident?"

Tom sighed. "No, it wasn't an accident. It wasn't natural either." He cleared his throat and offered Ava a nervous smile. "He was attacked, and the only thing the assailant went after was my father's eyes. The doctors think the injury sped up any mental decline that was there."

"That's terrible," Ava said, her voice soft and her face pale. "I'm so sorry both of you have had to suffer through this."

"Thanks," Tom smiled. He took a sip from the coffee. When he looked at Ava, his smile broadened. "I didn't lose my arm in the same attack."

Her cheeks darkened, and a rueful smile spread across her own face. "I was thinking of asking."

"I figured you were," Tom chuckled. "No, I lost it a little before that. There was an accident at a gas station. One of the pumps went, and before the emergency shut off could be hit, I lost my arm to shrapnel from the building itself."

"I'm not going to lie, you two have been through a lot."

Tom nodded. "Yeah. It's been a little rough at times."

Ava laughed, a clear, sweet sound that pleased him. She got to her feet.

"Rough at times," she repeated, shaking her head. "Most people would call that a little more than rough times, Tom."

He shrugged and smiled. "It is what it is. Thank you for the coffee, Ava."

"Everyone here thinks you're great," she told him. "You're the most devoted son we've seen. You're here all the time, you call us when you can't get in. Everyone in the unit wishes there were more family members involved like you. I know for a fact that some of our residents would be better off with more familial interaction. Come on up to the desk if you need anything."

"I will."

Tom watched as the young woman walked away. Then, he shifted his attention back to his father, who still sat in the patch of sunlight. Other residents walked around the ward, several more sat watching a television that played reruns of some sixties adventure show.

Tom set his coffee down on the table in front of him, removed his tablet from his bag, and opened up the page for the University of Connecticut. He needed to finish selecting his classes if he was going to get in for the next semester.

***

Tom was home long before six in the evening.

But there was work he needed to finish before he entertained any sort of company. Even if it was Frank.

He adjusted the protective rings once more, nodded and knew everything was as well as it could be. He set the box down in the center of the iron and salt rings, then reached in with his iron hook, flipping the box lid open as he had done with Oda.

But it was not Oda or anyone like Oda who stepped out. The ghost who looked at Tom from the confines of the barrier was an old man, and one who wore an expression of severe displeasure. The man would, Tom knew, kill him if given the chance.

Tom didn't plan on that.

"Good evening," Tom said, bowing. "My name is Tom, Mr. Alewife. I was hoping to ask you some questions."

Some of the displeasure slipped off the dead man's face. "To ask me some questions, young man?"

"Yes, sir."

"I didn't bury any treasure, you know," Mr. Alewife stated.

"I didn't think you had, sir."

"I don't know any great and terrible secrets, either."

"That's fine, sir."

"Well, I can't imagine what your questions might pertain to. You're not planning on torturing me, are you?" Mr. Alewife asked.

"Sir, I have no desire to do anything of the sort," Tom replied truthfully. "I have some questions I think you can help me with. Well, I hope you can help me with that."

Curiosity replaced the dead man's displeasure. "Color me intrigued, Tom. What are you wondering about?"

"I've read your history, sir," Tom began. "And I know you lost your older brother to dementia."

"I did," Mr. Alewife confirmed. "Is that what you want to know about? My brother?"

"Not specifically," Tom confessed. "I'm interested in how the disease progressed. I want to know what to look for from people who were close to it."

"I know I have been dead for some time," Mr. Alewife informed him. "Are you telling me that there's been no progress in all that time?"

"There has," Tom answered, nodding. "But I don't think there's enough about it. I need more."

"Why?" the dead man asked. "What concern do you have? Is it you? Are you afraid of being struck down with it so young?"

"No," Tom shook his head. "My father is suffering from it, sir. I know I won't be able to save him, but I'd like to ease his passing."

"Ah," the ghost replied. "That makes complete sense. I don't know how much you can gain from my brother's story, but if you're willing to listen, I am willing to talk."

"Thank you, sir," Tom said, letting out a shaky sigh of relief as he picked up his clipboard and pen. "What was the first sign of dementia you can remember, Mr. Alewife?"

✳ ✳ ✳

Stan thanked the driver, closed the door and stepped away from the car as the Uber left. He adjusted his grip on the handle of his suitcase and looked at the building Shane Ryan had sent him to.

The structure, which had once been a small church, was well-kept and well-loved. The paint was bright white, the windows shone, and the rose bushes around the property were neatly trimmed. Stan was impressed. He stood a moment longer, as if memorizing every aspect of the exterior, and then crossed the narrow country road. He climbed the steps, knocked on the door and waited.

"Hold on!" a man called from inside.

A moment later, the door opened, and Tom Daniels, Shane's associate, smiled at him.

"Stan?" Tom asked.

"Yes."

"Come on in," Tom said and stepped aside.

Stan entered the young man's home and took it in. Museum-quality display cases occupied the center of the large room, and similar shelves lined the walls. Bright lights illuminated the various items, and a curious, homey atmosphere settled around him.

"Do you want me to take your suitcase?" Tom asked, closing and securing the door.

"If you could show me where to put it, Tom, I would be happy to do so," Stan answered.

Tom smiled. "Follow me."

Stan did so, glancing from side to side at the cases and the protected items. Soon, he was shown to a spare bedroom, and as Tom flipped the light switch, Stan noticed the young man's hand.

10

"May I ask how you lost your hand?" he asked, placing the suitcase on the unmade bed.

Tom chuckled. "Not just the hand, it's just about the whole arm."

He knocked on his upper arm to prove his point. "As to how I lost it, well, that's a really, really long story. I don't think I can really tell it tonight. It's been a long day."

Stan nodded. "I understand."

"Do you drink tea, Stan?"

"It is my drink of choice."

Tom laughed. "Good. Come on, I'll put on some water to boil, and we can have a chat."

Stan nodded and followed Tom to the kitchen, a small, raised area where the pulpit must have once stood. As Tom prepared everything, Stan sat in a nearby chair, watching. The young man moved deftly in the kitchen, and there was no hint that his prosthetic arm was any sort of an impediment.

"Shane told me you need some help?" Tom said, and when he spoke Shane's name, Stan could hear a bit of anger in it.

"Should I not have come?" Stan asked. "I did not mean to cause any trouble."

"No," Tom sighed. "It's really not you. It's me. I'm still dealing with some issues between Shane and me. Do you know him well?"

"I admit that I do not."

"People die around him," Tom stated, his voice flat. "Lots of people."

"I understand."

Tom glanced at him, then nodded. "Yeah. You look like you do. Anyway, I like Shane. He's been there for me. Right now, though, I don't think I can be around him. A little too much death, if you can understand that."

"I can."

The tea kettle whistled, and Tom went to the stove. He clicked off the burner and asked over his shoulder, "So, what exactly are we looking for?"

Stan folded his hands on his lap and explained the situation.

CHAPTER 3
LOOK NOT TO HOPE

Ezra Pettigrew had allowed himself hubris.

Foolishly so, as was most often the case.

Robert shook his head. "I had hoped, sir, that with our withdrawal from Mason, we would have heard the last of Stan Owens."

Ezra sighed. "Apparently not, Robert. It seems that he is bent on vengeance."

Robert nodded.

"Which leads us to deciding what to do next. Do we think he will not find us?" Ezra asked.

Robert's brows furrowed. "No, I'm almost certain he will. From the brief report I had this morning, our hacker said this new look is far more in-depth. Definitely from someone with more skill than the previous searcher."

"Hmm." Ezra rubbed at his chin. "I doubt then that we're looking at Stan himself. Which means, of course, he will be able to act immediately on any information he is given."

"I don't think we'll move again, correct, sir?"

"Correct." Ezra frowned. "We should, I believe, make this place defensible."

Robert raised an eyebrow.

"Yes," Ezra continued.

"Security might draw attention," Robert stated. "Especially if we use physical security."

"That's true," Ezra smiled. "But that's not the security I was thinking of. I would like to make this a secure building, not with the living, but with the dead."

Robert shook his head. "I don't understand."

"We know that the dead draw power from electricity. If we were to hardline and protect our wires, this would stop the dead from drawing power. If we then secure each room using salt, lead and iron, we would have self-contained units where we could either place a ghost or keep one out of it."

"And if we restrict access," Robert said, catching on, "we can dictate what rooms will lead where."

"Exactly." Ezra picked up a glass of water, took a sip and then continued. "That should only be part of the defensive network."

"The best contain a mix of static and active," Robert advised. "A static defense here could allow us to send out living agents in search of Stan. We could even station the dead throughout the city to keep an eye out for him as well. This would be better than cameras. We wouldn't have to worry about getting caught setting them up."

"Yes." Ezra paused a moment before adding, "I was thinking of something rather dangerous and, well, not quite so legal."

Robert waited politely.

"You see," Ezra explained, "I've been having an issue obtaining the necessary ghosts."

"Yes," Robert frowned. "Morrigan doesn't seem to be fulfilling the orders quickly enough."

"And she's rather reticent about an idea of mine. I mentioned to her that there are a large number of violent individuals in the US, and perhaps, just perhaps, we could harvest some of them."

"To make our own violent ghosts?" Robert asked.

Ezra nodded.

"And they would be loyal to you," Robert continued.

"Either loyal out of duty or loyal out of fear," Ezra clarified. "Either one is acceptable. As long as they know I can control them and destroy them if necessary, I think the plan should work well. There will be hiccups, of course."

Robert smiled. "Every plan has hiccups, sir. It's the nature of the beast."

"True."

"And," Robert added, "this might be lucrative."

Ezra chuckled. "That is also true. I was mulling it over last night. I can't be the only person who needs a violent ghost every now and again. Morrigan seems to have a morality issue when it comes to cultivating and reaping violent ghosts. I don't."

"That's rather short-sighted of her," Robert muttered.

Ezra shrugged. "It is what it is, as they say. We can recognize it, Robert. We can achieve that goal and work towards it. I think it would be lucrative for us both."

"I agree, sir."

"Now," Ezra said, "let's shift away from the idea of the dead for a moment or two and focus on the living. We would need to hire some physical resources. I don't want any ex-military, however. I think that's where I went wrong with Winston. There's a sort of raw earthiness to Stan's violence. If we were to hire men on his own level, I think we would get a better result."

"Street fighters and thugs?" Robert asked.

"Yes, exactly. I know we used a few before. One pair of brothers sticks out in particular."

Robert laughed, nodding. "Oh, I know who you're talking about, sir. The Waverly brothers. They broke up a couple of strikes for you a few years ago. Really, stand-out work."

Ezra chuckled. "They certainly did work well. Do we still have their number on file?"

"We do, sir."

"Good," Ezra smiled. "Make the call to them your priority for the rest of the afternoon. I'd like to get a contract with them as soon as possible. Also, sound them out. See if there are any other people they might recommend working with."

"How many should we look to hire?"

"Let's say up to twenty," Ezra answered after a moment's pause. "I don't think we'll get that many or even need that many, but it wouldn't hurt. Better to have and not need than need and not have."

"Understood, sir," Robert said. "Should I start looking for contractors regarding the physical modifications to the building?"

Ezra nodded. "Yes. I'll reach out to Morrigan shortly. See if she has anything for us. If not violent, then at least trustworthy when it comes to relaying an early warning."

"I know the Waverly brothers were often working," Robert stated. "Should we offer an incentive if they're currently hired elsewhere?"

"Yes." Ezra rubbed at his chin. "Offer them ten percent more than whatever their contract price may be and tell them we'll offer the same amount to whoever currently holds their contract for allowing us to interrupt their work."

"Excellent, sir," Robert smiled. "I'll get right on it."

As Robert left the room, Ezra picked up his notepad and jotted down a rough estimate of the amount of ghosts he might need for the building and for an early warning system.

After that, he would need to call Morrigan.

CHAPTER 4
LOOKING FOR A BOOK

"Are you sure about this?"

Stan looked up from buttoning his suit coat.

"Yes," he assured Tom. "I am quite sure."

"I don't know if this ghost is aggressive or not," Tom continued. "All I know is that there's a ghost."

Stan forced himself to offer up a reassuring smile. "Tom, I am well acquainted with a variety of ghosts. If it is aggressive, I will be able to assist. And, I might add, it is the least I can do. You are helping me quite a bit."

"Okay," Tom grinned. "It's about a thirty-minute drive, and the man who told me about it, Herbert, said the key is under a brick by the side door."

They left the house and climbed into Tom's small pickup truck.

"Are you nervous?" Tom asked.

Stan frowned. "Why would I be?"

"I can only drive with one arm."

"That does not matter to me," Stan replied. "I dislike driving entirely. It is why I took an Uber."

"All the way from New Hampshire? I meant to ask you before about that."

Stan shook his head. "I used an Uber to Nashua, a bus from Nashua to Boston, the train from Boston to Mystic, and an Uber from Mystic to your home."

"Sounds straightforward."

"It was."

Tom glanced at him, smiled and started the truck. "Tell me about Mason, New Hampshire."

"It is a small town," Stan began and spoke of its history as they drove.

✱ ✱ ✱

The house looked as though it should be haunted.

A tall Victorian, the home spread across its lot and reached for the sky with three full stories. In the fading light of the day, Stan could not tell if the gray of the siding was intentional or a product of years beneath the sun. Ivy climbed the pillars and wrapped around the roof's edge. No light shone from the windows, and the unkempt lawn gave off an air of abandonment.

Tom parked and turned off the engine.

"Herbert said there's always been a ghost," he explained. "But lately, since Herbert's wife, Lauren, has been away, the ghost has been more active."

"Away?" Stan asked.

"She's in the Alzheimer's ward where my dad is," Tom said. "That's how I met Herbert. I overheard him talking with Lauren, trying to get her to talk about the ghost. Give him some sort of understanding as to how to deal with it."

"Was she able to?"

Tom shook his head. "She didn't remember Herbert that trip. I waited for him outside, explained who I was and what I used to do."

"Did he believe you?"

"No," Tom smiled. "Not at first. He thought I was trying to get money out of him. Not until I told him I didn't want any money, that I only wanted the ghost when I found it. He agreed to that."

"Did he want to know what you were going to do with the ghost?"

"Not at all," Tom answered. "He told me the ghost has been keeping him awake. Waiting till he fell asleep before making noise."

"That is not acceptable," Stan frowned. "A person should be able to sleep in their own home. What will you do with the ghost?"

Tom looked at him, confused, and then the young man's eyes widened. "Oh, man, I never told you, did I?"

"Told me what?"

"You saw everything in the house, right?" Tom asked.

"Your home? Yes."

"So, those are all haunted items," Tom explained. "I find haunted items, and I put them away for safekeeping. My dad and I inherited the collection and the building, and we've added pieces to it over the years. I don't do it often, not with getting ready for school and how rough the past year has been."

"That is understandable." Stan looked at the house through the window. "Our goal is to find the ghost, find the item the ghost is attached to, and safely bring it back to your home."

"That's it."

"You have a way to transport whatever the item is?" Stan asked.

"The cap on the truck bed," Tom answered, nodding toward the rear of the vehicle. "It's lined with lead and salt. We can secure the item back there."

"Excellent. Shall we go?"

"Let's," Tom chuckled, and they exited the vehicle.

The key was where Herbert had said it would be, and it took only a moment to gain access to the house.

They entered through a breezeway and then passed into the kitchen, turning on the light and revealing a room that had all the hallmarks of a man recently thrust into bachelorhood. Dirty pots and pans cluttered the counter, and a trash bag, overflowing with disposable plates and plastic flatware, stood in the corner. The refrigerator hummed and thumped in the corner, and Stan could well imagine how bare that appliance might be.

They passed from the kitchen, turning lights on as they went, into a narrow hallway that opened into a wider one. Stairs, broad enough to allow two people to climb them at once, reached up to the second floor. Large rooms opened off the main hallway, and Tom started on the left. The first room was a walk-in pantry, the second a sewing room, and the third a large dining room. They crossed the hall, entered the room, and found themselves in a large library. Books filled the cases that stretched from floor to ceiling.

The lights flickered.

Stan and Tom came to a stop.

Movement caught Stan's attention, and he looked to the right corner. A shape lingered in the darkness, watching.

Tom turned away from the shape and asked in a low voice, "Do you see it?"

"I do," Stan answered. In a louder voice, he said, "I am always impressed by personal libraries. They reveal much about the reader."

"These aren't Herbert's books," Tom informed him. "They belong to his wife."

The shape in the corner took a step forward.

"Ah." Stan shifted his position to look at the corner. "This would explain a great deal."

"Yup." Tom turned and faced the corner as well. He smiled and asked, "Are you the ghost Herbert's been complaining about?"

The dead person in the corner snorted, and Stan knew Tom had struck the right note with which to begin the conversation.

"He's done nothing but complain about me for fifty-three years," a female voice declared. "You would think he'd be done by now."

"Apparently not," Tom said. "My name is Tom Daniels, and this is Stan Owens. May my friend and I sit down?"

The ghost hesitated, then answered, "Yes."

A single chair and a low couch served as seats, and so Stan sat alongside Tom on the couch. The chair, Stan supposed, belonged to Lauren. Sitting there would have been a mistake.

Stan appreciated how well Tom was handling the situation.

"What brings you here, other than Herbert's complaints?" the ghost asked.

"That's all," Tom answered. "He was wondering if we could help him."

The ghost shook her head and moved a few steps closer. The lights flickered but remained on. "I'm not leaving. I'm waiting until Lauren comes back. We have lots of books to read still."

"I'm sorry," Tom said, his voice gentling. "Lauren isn't coming back."

The dead woman became plain to see.

She was short, perhaps no more than five feet tall and was, without any question, extremely attractive. Her clothing marked her as having lived in the Victorian period, and her youthful face showed she had died in her early twenties.

"What has he done to her?" the dead woman demanded.

"Nothing," Tom assured the ghost. "Lauren is sick."

The dead woman shook her head.

"She has become forgetful," Tom continued. "To the point that it's dangerous for her to be alone in the house. It was, from what I read, even dangerous to leave her alone in a room."

"Not when she was here," the ghost retorted. "Not when she was with me."

"Were you with her all the time?" Stan asked.

The dead woman shook her head and lowered her chin. "No. There were some days when she was too afraid of me. She forgot that she knows me."

"How long have you known her?" Stan asked.

"Since before she was born," the ghost smiled. "I watched her mother's pregnancy and was thrilled when Lauren was brought home. I have been with her ever since. We have always read together. We have always been together. I don't want her to die."

"I understand," Tom told her, and Stan heard the sincerity in the young man's voice. "She's safe where she is now. She is taken care of and watched around the clock. There are special nurses and doctors who are there to make certain she doesn't hurt herself."

"And that cannot happen here?" the ghost asked.

Stan shook his head. "It costs too much."

The ghost frowned. "Despite my dislike for Herbert, you cannot accuse him of being a miser. Especially when it comes to Lauren. He will spend his last dime on her, even if it means he would go hungry."

"He may have to," Tom told her. "Where he has placed her is an expensive institution. They will do their best to ease her passing."

"That will leave me here with Herbert." The ghost shook her head. "That is unacceptable. I dislike the man. How can I bear to spend the rest of his days with him? He doesn't read! He sits in front of that infernal box and watches whatever nonsense plays across it."

"You could come with me," Tom told her.

The dead woman blinked. "And where would that be?"

"I own a small home," Tom stated. "And there are a lot of ghosts there. I keep them safe behind leaded glass. Some like to come out and speak. Others have no wish to be bothered. I check in on everyone once a month. One or two drift around the property, but they mostly stay close by."

She looked at him, then inspected her nails before asking, "Do you read?"

Tom grinned. "Every chance I get."

A small smile played across the ghost's face. "And what do you read?"

"History, philosophy, classics."

"And would you be averse to reading with a compatriot?" she asked. "Perhaps even discussing the books when we have finished them?"

"I would like nothing more," Tom told her. "I used to do that with my father."

"Then," she said, straightening up, "I would like to go home with you, Tom Daniels. If you are willing to put up with another ghost."

"I am," he answered. "What's your name?"

"My name?" she smiled. "Oh, it has been a long time since someone asked me for my name. I am Katerina Potts."

"Well, Katerina," Tom got to his feet, "what is your item?"

"It is Lauren's favorite book, of course," Katerina smiled. "*The House of Seven Gables* by Nathaniel Hawthorne. Come, I will show you where it sits. It takes pride of place, as my father would have said."

Stan watched Tom follow the ghost to a shelf and then point out the volume in question. Tom took it down gently, and Stan could see the appreciative smile on Katerina's face.

"You do know how to handle books," the dead woman nodded. "Lauren would have liked you."

"I like books," Tom admitted.

"There is liking books, Mr. Daniels," she replied, "and there is loving books. You, young sir, are of the latter category."

Tom nodded. "Are you ready to leave?"

"Quite," Katerina answered. She shifted her attention to Stan. "Do you read as well, Mr. Owens?"

"It is one of the few pleasures I allow myself," he told her.

"Good."

Katerina looked from one man to the other and then faded from view.

It was, Stan knew, time to leave.

CHAPTER 5
SIBLINGS

Morrigan tapped her spoon three times on the edge of her coffee mug and then set it down to dry on her napkin.

"Any luck with Pettigrew?" Lisbeth asked, sipping at her own coffee.

"No," Morrigan sighed. "He's becoming a nuisance."

Her sister frowned. "Are you going to cut him off?"

"Soon. Very soon." Morrigan took a drink, frowned, and picked up the sugar container. She shook it thrice, lifted her spoon and stirred the sugar in from left to right, then right to left, and lastly, left to right again. Once more, she tapped it three times on the edge and returned it to the napkin. "He left a message yesterday, asking me to return his call. He is, as he put it, 'in need of your services, Ms. Morrigan.'"

Lisbeth raised an eyebrow. "No 'please' or any sort of pleasantry?"

Morrigan shook her head.

Lisbeth snorted. "You should find one to put an end to him."

"No," she replied. "I can't do that."

Lisbeth rolled her eyes. "You can. You just won't."

"You are correct," Morrigan smiled at her younger sister. "It is not something I would be able to live with."

"But you send him ghosts," Lisbeth retorted. "Violent ghosts. Many of whom are quite comfortable with killing."

"And therein is the plausible deniability factor," she stated. "I sell him the ghosts. What he does with them after is on his head and his head alone. Until he tells me he is planning on murdering a specific individual, I will not act."

"Seems a pretty thin excuse to sell the dead," Lisbeth smirked.

Morrigan chuckled and nodded her head in agreement. "You are absolutely right about that. It is a thin excuse, but it does help."

"What about your new beau," Lisbeth winked. "Does he help, too?"

"Not like that," Morrigan answered, and she was surprised to feel the heat of embarrassment rush through her.

"Really?" Lisbeth frowned. "You, um, you haven't had any quality alone time together?"

"No," Morrigan repeated. "Not like that."

"Wow. When did you take your vows?"

"What vows?" Morrigan asked, flustered.

"Of celibacy?" Lisbeth snickered.

"Very funny." Morrigan sighed, shaking her head. "It's strange. The relationship is just sort of cruising along. It's not like either one of us is making sure it's slow. That's just the way it's unfolding. I kind of like it."

"So, no butterflies or anything?" Lisbeth asked, reclining in her seat.

"No, plenty of butterflies," Morrigan replied. "Every time I set eyes on him or talk to him on the phone."

"Must be nice," Lisbeth muttered. "I don't have a boyfriend."

"You stabbed your last boyfriend," Morrigan reminded her. "Twice, if I'm not mistaken."

"He deserved it."

"I don't doubt it." Morrigan smiled. "However, that tends to cause an issue with any other men who might be considering a relationship with you."

Lisbeth shrugged. "Something to worry about some other time. Still, I am kind of jealous."

"I'm sorry."

"Don't be." Lisbeth shifted in her seat. "So, when are you going to tell Mom and Dad?"

"I'm not," Morrigan answered. "And I'd appreciate it if you didn't. I don't want to listen to Mom harp on about how she's not a grandmother yet."

"I kind of remember you telling her you didn't want to have kids," Lisbeth stated.

"You would be remembering correctly." Morrigan sipped her coffee. "Mom and Dad didn't do such a bang-up job with us, so, you know, I don't want to risk being as bad. Or worse."

"Anyway," Lisbeth yawned, "we've gossiped, we've complained, and we've had our coffee. What's next?"

Morrigan looked at her sister and smiled.

Lisbeth grinned back at her. "Who else can you trust, huh?"

"Just you."

"That's right, just me," Lisbeth nodded. "So, what's next?"

"I'd like you to take a trip for me," Morrigan answered.

"Where to?"

"Connecticut."

Lisbeth raised an eyebrow. "You talking about the beautiful side of Connecticut, or am I going to hang out in some dive of a town that hasn't seen a good day since Teddy Roosevelt was president?"

Morrigan laughed. "I want you to go to Norwich. It's right next to Foxwoods and Mohegan Sun, so I'll probably put you up in one of those."

"Ooh, this sounds interesting," Lisbeth smiled. "Tell me more."

"There's supposed to be a collector around there. The information is kind of sketchy. I have two separate accounts." Morrigan picked up a notebook and read from it. "According to some sources, the owner is an old man. No real information on his name or anything else. Other sources say it's owned by a middle-aged man and his son. The only thing I know for certain is that whoever owns the collection doesn't make themselves known. They'll pick up a piece here or there, then tuck it away."

"Are you looking to purchase the whole collection or just parts of it?" Lisbeth asked.

"First, I want to establish that the collection is even there," Morrigan replied. "When we know that, we can approach the owner and see if they are interested. We definitely need to establish a relationship with them first."

"You want me to prowl around any of the local antique shops and such when I'm down there?"

"Of course," Morrigan grinned. "That would be a waste of a trip if you didn't."

"It would be." Lisbeth stretched and looked around. "This is going well, sis."

"It really is. Couldn't do it without you."

"I know," Lisbeth winked. "And you won't have to do it without me. This is better than any job I've ever had. Probably better than any I ever will have. Thank you."

"Thank you."

The sisters stood, and they cleared their dishes with an ease and rhythm they'd had since childhood.

CHAPTER 6
NECESSARY INFORMATION

For three days and three nights, Stan lived with Tom.

The young man was quiet, polite and witty, and Stan enjoyed his company, even though it reminded him of Adam, who remained in a coma in Nashua.

There was nothing he could do for Adam, and that knowledge ate at him. Stan reflected on the ghost in the stairwell at the hospital and the brutal reality of Adam's lingering existence.

Stan shifted in bed and looked out the window into the night sky and the sliver of moon that hung among the stars. He lay there for several minutes, then got out of bed and dressed. For the first time, he withdrew a large belt from his suitcase. The belt's thick leather and heavy steel buckle were an uncomfortable reminder of his past, but, as the old saying went, it was better to have and not need than need and not have. And he would have to reacclimate his body to wearing the heavy accessory. The police would frown on brass knuckles, not so much a stout belt and matching buckle.

When he exited his room, Stan saw Tom's door was closed. The sound of a keyboard clacking and softly spoken words escaped into the hall. Tom could type deftly with his one good hand and occasionally used the speech-to-text function as well. Once more, Stan found himself admiring Tom's ability to overcome adversity.

Stan passed through the large display room, pausing only for a moment beside a sealed bookcase that contained a number of books, including the newest one recovered from Herbert's home. It would be enjoyable, Stan realized, to sit and speak with Katerina.

Still, there were the dead wandering the property, and he would like to speak with them as well.

Stan reached the door and eased it open, careful of squeaking hinges. He did not wish to alarm Tom. The young man had started a pair of online classes and another set in person. He would need all the quiet he could in order to focus.

A chill breeze swept over Stan as he stepped outside, closing the door behind him. He could smell fall in the air, and he thought of Gwen. A smile slipped onto his face, and he wished he could sit with her in the darkness, waiting for autumn to arrive and settle in over the land. While he tolerated the other seasons, he enjoyed autumn most. He could remember trick-or-treating with his mother, the joy of dressing like a Star Wars character and rambling through the neighborhoods, seeking out the best candy.

But he only had a few of those he could recall.

Everything else had been stolen from him by his granduncle.

Stan paused for a moment and wondered if he should enlist the aid of Philomena when it came time to deal with Ezra Pettigrew.

With a shake of his head, he decided he couldn't. Philomena was strong, and he had no doubt if she put her mind to it, she would find a way to harm him. Especially after he had finished exacting revenge on Pettigrew for the death of Kenny. Stan and his dead grandaunt had come to a sort of mutual understanding, but its foundation rested firmly on Kenny, who had been not only Stan's friend but Philomena's godson as well.

Vengeance only lasted so long as a prop for the relationship between the living and the dead.

Stan let those thoughts slip away as he stepped out into what had once been a small parking lot for Tom's home, which, in its previous life, had been a church. He could only imagine what type of congregation had called this building their spiritual home. Was it a group of Lutherans or perhaps Congregationalists? It did not have the hallmarks of a Catholic church. It could be placed squarely among the Protestants.

"Who are you?"

Stan looked up and found a young woman standing a short distance from him. Her pale face, the night dress that reached the top of her bare feet, and the fact that he could see through her informed him as to her status as a ghost.

"I am Tom's friend," he answered the dead woman. "My name is Stan. May I know yours?"

"No."

Stan nodded his acceptance. "Am I allowed to walk here?"

"No."

"That is unfortunate." He sighed and looked to his left and then to his right. He and the ghost were alone. Stan stepped over to one of two wooden chairs, unbuttoned his suitcoat and sat down.

"I didn't say you could sit," the ghost snapped.

"I did not ask."

A smirk spread across her face, and she moved closer. "Good."

Stan folded his hands over his lap and looked at her, wondering what questions might be appropriate to ask the dead woman.

"You dress strangely for the times," she remarked.

"I do," he acknowledged.

"Why?"

Stan blinked. "That is a fair question. These clothes remind me of a time long before I was born."

"Why would that be important?"

"Because my troubles had not existed then," Stan replied.

"You didn't even exist then."

Stan nodded. "That is exactly the point."

"Hmm. You remind me of men from my time," she told him. "They would dress like that. They had cufflinks, too. The ones who were better off, at least."

"I am not better off," Stan said, raising his arms up and pulling the coat's arms back slightly to reveal his shirt cuffs and the links. "But I do enjoy wearing cufflinks. They are part of that time."

The dead woman crossed over, sat down in the chair opposite him and asked, "Why are you here?"

"Tom is helping me," he answered. "I am seeking a man who has killed one of my friends."

"And what will you do if you find him?"

"I will do my best to kill him," Stan informed her.

She winced. "You shouldn't."

"I know."

She peered at him. "But you'll still kill him?"

"Yes."

"Do you believe in forgiveness?"

"For some, but not for all."

"And where do you fall in that category?" she asked, fixing an intense look upon him.

"Unforgivable," he said, a bit softly, as if to himself.

"Do you believe that?"

"I do, unfortunately." He shifted his gaze to the dirt parking lot, where grass had long ago begun to take it back.

"What would help you believe you could be forgiven?"

"Nothing," he told her. "Not a single thing."

The door opened, and Tom stepped out.

"Miss," Tom greeted.

The ghost stood and offered a short nod to both of them. "Good evening, gentlemen. It was a pleasure to meet you, Stan. Perhaps I will see you again before you leave."

Once the dead woman had left, Tom took her seat and shook his head. "She usually doesn't talk to anyone."

"That does not surprise me," Stan replied. "She did not strike me as overly friendly when she first spoke."

Tom nodded.

They sat in silence for a short time, then Tom asked, "Were you having trouble sleeping?"

"Yes."

"Something in the house?"

"No," Stan answered. "Something in the past. Nothing more."

"Got it." Tom yawned. "Well, I managed to get information on Ezra Pettigrew."

Stan turned fully in his seat to look at Tom. "That was fast."

Tom grinned. "I'm a little quicker with the internet than Shane is, not to throw any shade at him."

Stan frowned. "Shade?"

"Slander, talk down about," Tom answered. "Sorry. Little bit of slang there."

"You have no reason or need to apologize," Stan assured him. "I am old, and I am unaware of newer terminology."

"Okay," Tom smiled. "So, yes, I found some information. I still haven't quite located where he is, but I managed to get a hold of pictures of him and his office staff."

"May I see them?"

"That's why I came out here," Tom nodded.

They went back inside and into Tom's room. When Tom motioned for him to sit, Stan did so. He found himself looking at several images on Tom's laptop. All the photos were of the same three people. The pictures were taken in different locations, and at different times of the year, but the images looked recent. Possibly taken within the last three or four years.

Stan studied the photos for a few minutes. The tallest man appeared to be the oldest, and he was always flanked on either side by a younger man and woman. The man in the center looked as though he might have been taken out of a sixties or seventies advertisement for an executive. His silver hair was trimmed short, his features were broad and pleasant, and he carried himself with a certain self-assuredness. While both his companions were younger, they did not dress as well, and their demeanor showed their subservience to the man in the center.

"This is Pettigrew," Tom said, pointing at the older man. "And this is a man named Robert and a woman named Abigail. They are his main support structure. I did a little more digging, and it seems they've been with him for at least five or six years."

Stan leaned forward, frowning. "I have seen this man. The younger one."

"Where?"

"In Mason," Stan told him. "And recently, too. He stood out, though not as much as others have. He must have been there on orders from Ezra Pettigrew."

"That would make sense."

"Will you be able to find out more?" Stan asked.

Tom grinned. "Without a doubt. I'll get on it in the morning."

"Thank you, Tom." Stan got to his feet. "This will help me sleep."

"Good." Tom's grin faded. "Get some rest, and I'll see you in the morning."

Stan nodded, left the room and returned to his own. As he undressed and climbed into bed, he thought of Gwen and when he would see her again.

CHAPTER 7

GATHERING GOODS AND ASSISTANCE

Morrigan still hadn't returned his phone call, and Ezra found himself growing increasingly frustrated with the woman. Such failure at basic customer service was not how you managed a successful business. Ezra knew. He had run several businesses and looked forward to running more as his life continued. What he did not want to do was deal with people who failed at customer service.

Setting aside his frustration, he picked up his phone and called Morrigan again.

She answered it on the third ring, her voice distant and cold. "Good morning, Mr. Pettigrew."

That was not a good sign.

"Hello, Morrigan." Ezra forced himself to be cheerful. "How are you?"

"Tolerable," she answered.

"I hope your day gets better then," he told her. "I was wondering if we might discuss business."

"What other reason would there be for a call?"

Ezra cleared his throat. "True. Well, I was hoping to purchase several ghosts from you."

"I'm afraid that my stock of violent ghosts is exceptionally low," she remarked. "I have not had the opportunity to replace them."

"I'm not looking just for violent ghosts," he told her. "I'm also hoping to acquire some ghosts who excel in observation, those who can be trusted to watch and report."

"I don't know that I have any of that particular variety," she replied. "It's generally not a category that I put the dead into. How many would you be looking for at this time?"

"To begin with, I would like five. I need to establish a secure perimeter, and I believe the dead would serve me best for that."

"I will get back to you in three days," Morrigan stated. "By that time, I will know how many I have in stock who can carry out such a task."

"Three days?" Ezra frowned. "Can't you make it any sooner?"

"I can make it five," she replied, her tone harsh. "Perhaps ten days?"

Ezra hid his anger. "No. I'm sorry. I didn't mean to pressure you."

"Mr. Pettigrew, that is exactly what you meant to do. If I say three days, I mean three days. If you do not understand the constraints on a business such as mine, then I expect you to take your business elsewhere."

"Three days it is," Ezra grumbled, and she ended the call.

He held the phone for a moment, fighting the urge to hurl it against the wall.

✳ ✳ ✳

The cell phone flashed as it rang on the edge of the pool table.

"Somebody's calling," Hazen observed.

"Somebody can wait," Ethan replied and took his shot.

It was, unlike his pistol shooting, a terrible shot. The six ball glanced off the nine, hit the rail, spun back and struck the cue ball, sending that barreling into the far pocket.

"Wow," Hazen said.

"Shut it," Ethan sighed, setting the pool cue on the table. He picked up his phone and answered it without bothering to look at the number. "Go ahead."

"Mr. Ethan Waverly?" a voice asked.

"Yup," he answered, walking to his chair and dropping down into it.

"You sound familiar."

"My name is Robert."

Ethan snapped his fingers. "Oh, yeah! Strikebreaker job. What's up, my man?"

"I have another job for you and your brother, if you're up to it."

Ethan frowned. "We're kind of under contract right now, Robert. Working for Big Mike. You know him?"

Robert paused, then replied, "I've heard the name. Mr. Waverly—"

"Ethan."

"Ethan," Robert corrected himself. "I have been told I can offer you and your current contract holder a significant bonus if he lets you out of your contract, at least for a short period."

"That so?"

"It is." Robert then relayed a number that made Ethan smile.

"Are you serious?" Ethan asked, chuckling.

"I am."

"And Big Mike would get a cut of that?"

"No," Robert answered. "He would get that same amount."

Ethan let out a low whistle and Hazen glanced up from the daily paper's crossword. He raised an eyebrow, and Ethan held up a finger.

"I'm pretty sure Big Mike would go for it," Ethan said. "I just have to check with him."

"Of course," Robert replied. "The number I'm calling from is the best way to contact me."

"Good. I should have an answer by tonight. Tomorrow morning at the latest," Ethan informed him. "Thanks for thinking of us, Robert."

"You did excellent work. My employer has not forgotten that."

Ethan ended the call, put the phone down for a moment and looked at his brother.

"Who was that?" Hazen asked.

"The guy who hired us a year or so ago to do some work on those employees who were striking up in Willimantic. Remember?"

Hazen frowned, shrugged and said, "Sort of. Were those the guys we used the axe handles on?"

"Yup."

"Okay. Yeah, I remember. He wants us for a job even though we're working for Big Mike?" Hazen asked.

"You got it."

"How's that going to work?" Hazen put his crossword down. "Big Mike's not a fan of letting help out."

"Big Mike's a fan of money," Ethan grinned. "And this guy offered us a lot of money and the same amount to Big Mike for letting us work as freelancers for a bit."

"How much is a lot?"

Ethan told his brother and laughed when Hazen swore in surprise.

"When are you going to talk to Big Mike?" Hazen asked.

"Right now," Ethan answered and picked up the phone.

CHAPTER 8
A PLEASANT CONVERSATION

"How does this work?" Stan asked.

"Here." Tom clicked on the mouse, and a window opened on the laptop. "This is a Zoom link. I sent it to your friend Gwen, and she's set up a meeting for you. As soon as she lets you in, you can start talking."

Stan glanced over his shoulder. "I do not understand."

"This," Tom replied, pointing at a small, black circle in the center of the white frame around the laptop's screen. "Is a camera. When you get let in, you'll see yourself and you'll see Gwen. The volume is up, everything is good to go. Look, she's letting you in."

Stan saw the screen shifting, and a moment later, he found himself looking at Gwen in her office. He smiled as she did the same.

"How's the audio?" she asked. "Can you hear me?"

Stan saw himself in a small screen tucked into the corner. Tom appeared in it, saying, "Hi Gwen, I'm Tom. Audio and video are good on this end."

"Nice to meet you, Tom," she smiled. "Thank you for doing this."

"Of course. Enjoy your chat."

Tom left the room, and Stan focused on Gwen.

"I miss you," he told her, and her cheeks reddened.

"I miss you, too," she replied. "How long are you going to be away?"

"I am not certain," he sighed. "Unfortunately, it is difficult to know."

She nodded. "Well, at least we can talk and see each other. It'll be better when you're home, though. We can grab some coffee and go down to the oval if the weather is still good."

"I'd like that," Stan replied. "How are you doing?"

"Tired," she told him. "A couple of my clients moved on from needing intensive therapy, so it opened up some time slots. That means I have a pair of new customers. It's always interesting and challenging to take on someone new, but it's tiring, too." She waved dismissively. "But my stuff is boring. What are you up to down there?"

"Research," Stan answered. "I wish it were something more interesting, but it is not."

"I think it's too bad the information you need isn't digitized," Gwen said. "That way, you would be home. Closer to me."

Stan felt the comfortable flush rush through him. "Yes. I would prefer to be closer to you, too."

"So, other than research, are you doing anything exciting?"

Stan shook his head. "We have looked at some books, and Tom has discussed with me his studies. He is focused on Alzheimer's and its effects. His father is suffering from it, and Tom often goes to the nursing home to visit him."

"Is his father really old?" she asked. "Tom looks like a young man."

"His father is younger than I am," Stan replied. "I have not met his father, and I doubt I am likely to do so. I feel for Tom, though. I know what it is like to lose your father."

"I know you do."

They were quiet for a moment, and then Gwen smiled. "Tell me what you're going to do tomorrow and what it's like there."

"Tomorrow," Stan began, and he told her all about what he hoped to accomplish.

CHAPTER 9

LOOKING FOR SOME HELP

"Big Mike gave the okay?" Hazen asked.

Ethan nodded. "Yup. Happy to, in fact. Guess he ended up talking to Robert, who told him he was looking for a few more guys."

"Strange. But, whatever. Do we get a finder's fee or anything?"

Ethan snorted and shook his head.

"Huh. Kind of think we should."

"Don't think," Ethan replied. "You weaken the nation."

Hazen flipped him off and held the door open to Odie's Bar. The curious funk that gave Odie's its potent name washed over them and caused the brothers' eyes to momentarily water.

"When is he going to clean this place?" Ethan winced, walking into the semi-darkness.

"He did last week," Hazen answered. "Deep clean, too. Someone was telling him it's sunk into the joints of the building now. You'd have to strip the whole thing down and start over. And even then, that might not do the trick."

Ethan grunted and made his way to the bar.

Tabby, dressed in clothes that had stopped fitting her fifty pounds earlier, looked up and flashed a smile made entirely of dentures.

"The Waverly boys," she greeted, some of the syllables whistling past her false teeth. "Been a hot minute since we've seen you in here."

"Been busy," Hazen stated as he and Ethan took seats at the bar.

"Lots of work," Ethan agreed.

"How's Carol and that little girl of yours?" Tabby asked, drawing a pair of draft beers for them.

"Good," Ethan smiled. "Thanks for asking."

"And what about you?" she asked, turning her attention to Hazen. "You hooked up yet?"

He shook his head. "No way. I enjoy my freedom."

Tabby snorted. "Lack of responsibility isn't the same as freedom. Anyway, what are you boys doing in here? Didn't expect to see you anytime soon, not with you working for Big Mike."

"We're actually here because Big Mike sent us," Ethan told her. "We're looking to hire on some extra muscle for a bit."

Tabby raised an eyebrow that was more liner than it was hair. "How much more?"

"Up to fifteen," Ethan answered.

"I don't know if you'll find fifteen guys in here," Tabby said. "It's been thin, real thin. Couple of guys were just sent back to York prison, and the Hernandez brothers were deported to Mexico."

"They're Puerto Rican," Ethan frowned. "How could they get deported to Mexico?"

"They upset the state prosecutor," Tabby replied. "He made sure their paperwork got shuffled. I think they'll be back in a month or two. If not here, probably in PR."

Hazen shook his head. "That's a shame. I was kind of hoping to get the Hernandez brothers on board. They don't shy away from much."

"That's why they're locked up again," Ethan observed.

Hazen shrugged and took a drink.

"Anyway," Ethan sighed, wrapping his hands around his glass. "Talk to me, Tabby. Anybody looking good?"

"If you hang around another hour or two, you'll get a few bites," she suggested. "Maybe two or three. Stay later, there'll be even more. Honestly, though, you might have to go down to New London. I know some of those sailors think they're hot stuff. They try to work as bouncers."

Ethan shook his head. "No, we won't hire anybody who doesn't have some time under their belt. Keeps 'em honest, you know?"

"Yup."

Ethan shifted in his seat and looked at Hazen. "What do you think? Try to grab a couple here and then move on?"

"I say we give it a couple hours at least," Hazen offered up. "I mean, worst case scenario, we go and try another bar. But I think we'll be good."

"Yeah?" Ethan asked.

Hazen nodded. "Yup. Pretty sure everyone we need will show up here at some point in the night. It's payday, and most guys will be in here getting a few drinks in before the weekend."

Ethan grinned at his brother's logic, took a drink and made himself comfortable. They needed to wait, and he might as well enjoy it.

Hazen's head hurt, and the rumble of the jukebox didn't make it any better. Ethan had left at seven to pick up Mia, and he wasn't back yet. Hazen knew Carol was probably giving Ethan a hard time, and that wasn't anything new. She'd been after him since Mia was born to find a decent job that wouldn't land him in prison.

But Ethan, like Hazen, wasn't made for a decent job.

They did dirty work for a good price. The brothers were paid well, and they both enjoyed the violence. Sometimes, it wasn't anything more than intimidation, which bored them, but other times, they could get creative.

He reached for his glass, saw it was close to empty and motioned to Tabby for a refill.

"How are you even sitting in that chair?" she asked, getting him a fresh beer.

"I don't think about it," he answered.

Tabby snorted and shook her head. "How'd you do with that list of yours?"

"Good," he told her. "Really good. I've got eleven names on the paper here, and I think I'm going to call it a night after this beer. I had hoped for maybe eight; I didn't think I'd get eleven. Guess I can thank the economy for that one. Boys are asking for half up front, which is fine for me since I'm not the one paying them."

Tabby chuckled. "Well, good for you, then. Think Big Mike will be happy?"

Hazen glanced down at the list, nodded and answered, "Yeah. I think he'll be really happy with the names here. Especially when he gets paid for them."

"We all like to get paid," she remarked.

Hazen raised his glass and grinned. "Yes, we do."

CHAPTER 10
ARMORING THE KEEP

The sound of construction work filled the offices and set Ezra's teeth on edge.

A faint knock sounded on the door, and Abigail opened it a moment later. Her face mirrored his own frustration. She carried a cup of coffee and a fresh pastry, and she placed them both on the desk.

"I baked scones this morning," she told him. "I thought you might appreciate one, Mr. Pettigrew."

"You are absolutely correct, Abigail," he smiled. "Thank you for your thoughtfulness."

"You're welcome."

"How is it in your office?" he asked, picking up the scone and taking a small bite. He tasted apricot and sighed, enjoying the flavor.

"A little louder than this," she remarked. "But nothing unbearable, sir."

Ezra raised an eyebrow, swallowed his food and stated, "Abigail, there's nothing you need to do here today. Go home. Take a day off, go to a museum or a movie. You don't need to listen to this."

She shook her head. "Maybe I'll go out on my break and buy a pair of those noise-canceling headphones people are always talking about. Is that okay?"

"Of course, it is. We can go through the messages later when it doesn't sound like the world is ending outside our doors." A loud squeal punctuated the air, and he winced. "In fact, Abigail, why don't you go now and grab yourself a pair of them? No need to wait until your break."

She nodded, offered a tight smile by way of thanks, and left the room, holding the door open a moment for Robert to enter.

Robert appeared haggard, and Ezra hoped it was the noise of construction and nothing more that served as the source of the man's tiredness.

"Sit down, please," Ezra told him.

Robert nodded and dropped heavily into the proffered chair.

"Are you all right?" Ezra asked.

"As well as can be," Robert replied. "I had a long night. Terrible nightmares about my wife's passing. Then, a drunken but profitable call around midnight. I heard back from the Waverly brothers."

"And?"

Robert managed a smile. "They found another eleven men of questionable morale but definite skills when taking violence into consideration. We have a total of thirteen now."

Ezra chuckled. "An even baker's dozen, as the saying goes."

"Yes."

"I want you to take the rest of the day off," Ezra told him and shook his head as Robert frowned. "No. You're exhausted. Even if you just find a place nearby to sleep, do that. If you could convince Abigail, too, I would appreciate it. Neither of you need to suffer through this."

"We're suffering happily," Robert replied. "I would rather be here than home, Mr. Pettigrew. I suspect it's the same with Abigail."

Ezra could only nod.

"Did you hear back from Morrigan?" Robert asked.

"No," Ezra answered. "But I did call her. She's supposed to return my call and tell me whether she might have any dead who fit my needs."

A loud drill cut through their conversation, causing Ezra and Robert to wince simultaneously. The noise subsided a moment later, and the two men looked at each other before chuckling.

"Fortunately," Ezra sighed with a shake of his head, "that only happens every so often. However, it's why I want you and Abigail to leave. You don't need to work in this environment. Not for the whole day."

"I don't believe we'd be able to come back later," Robert reminded him. "We have three shifts scheduled in order to get the building secure."

Ezra nodded. "Yes, that's true. Do you think we can trust the Waverlys to establish a proper cordon around the city, or should we take that upon ourselves?"

"I think we should trust the Waverlys. Most of the men they picked are locals. They'll know what's out of place, and I'll be sure to get photos of Stan Owens out to them. I hope that by the time they're established, we'll have the ghosts, too," Robert added.

"That is my hope as well."

Loud, muffled voices pierced the walls, and Ezra caught the word "Reduction" but nothing more.

"Robert," Ezra said, getting to his feet, "gather up Abigail, would you? I do believe it's time for us to have a business lunch."

Ezra was rewarded with a look of appreciative thanks, and Robert left the room. As the man did so, Ezra put on his coat and patted his pockets to make certain his wallet and keys were in their proper places. With that done, he left the office and met his two staff members in the outer office.

"Is there anywhere in particular either of you might like to go?" Ezra asked, wincing at the sound of a circular saw ripping through the air.

Robert shook his head and picked up his laptop as Abigail stated, "Anywhere, Mr. Pettigrew. Anywhere but here."

"Agreed," Ezra nodded, and he led the way out of the office.

Morrigan sat in her chair and looked at the secured briefcase in front of her. Within its steel and iron-laced confines rested 15 items. All were haunted, and each ghost had agreed to watch and report. Nothing more.

When everything was said and done, Morrigan would find a way to retrieve them. She might need to enlist the aid of her sister for it, but that would be fine. It would keep the younger woman out of trouble, which was something she desperately needed.

Morrigan stood up and grasped the case by its handle. It was light and gave no hint of the deadly burden within it. She knew the ghosts would be diligent and do as they were told. She had selected them for their intelligence and determination, not for any violent or murderous intent. Morrigan had few of those left, and no more would be going to Ezra Pettigrew.

In fact, this shipment would be the last to Mr. Pettigrew.

Morrigan wanted no more of his nonsense.

Chapter 11
MISS

Stan finished his cup of tea, washed the cup and the saucer, and then left the house. He paused outside the door to turn up the collar on his suitcoat and then proceeded through the parking lot and into a small field. Above him, the half-moon shone, providing enough light to see the land around him and little else.

Stan slipped his hands into his pockets and followed a well-trodden path that led around the perimeter of the field. It was one made by Tom, and the young man used it daily. Stan did so at night when Tom was wont to complete schoolwork and continue the quest for where Ezra Pettigrew was hiding.

When he was only a hundred yards or so from the house, Miss appeared on his left. She floated beside him, keeping pace as he walked.

"You're a strange man, Stan," she spoke after a minute of silence.

"You are not the first to say so."

She flashed him a small smile. "Why are you strange?"

"A combination of factors, I suppose," he answered. "Upbringing, natural predisposition, and my experiences."

"Do you always answer so literally?"

Stan nodded. "I find it is easiest for me."

"Have you any new information on your victim?"

Stan raised an eyebrow but did not argue with her over the choice of words. "No. Nothing, yet. I hope to have some soon, however."

They continued without speaking until they reached the halfway point.

"Have you always seen the dead?" she asked.

He shook his head.

She waited a moment, then, when she realized he wasn't going to offer up more, pressed on. "Will you tell me?"

Stan glanced at her, considered the question and replied, "No. It is not a pleasant memory. Nor is the time after the birth of the ability pleasant to remember. Suffice to say, I was no longer a child and had seen enough of the world."

Miss frowned but held her tongue.

"Why do you walk at night?" she asked after he had begun a second lap.

"It helps me keep my thoughts clear," he told her. "There are times when it is difficult for me to think. Walking allows my mind to wander."

"You walked several miles last night."

"I am not surprised." He looked about the field and caught a glimpse of several other ghosts. The shapes were indistinct, and some appeared as little more than clumps of low-lying fog.

"They wonder about you," Miss stated. "They see you and know you can see them. None understand why you are not trying to interact."

"I respect their privacy," Stan replied. "You told me you did not wish to give your name, and so I can respect that. Just because you are dead, Miss, does not mean your wishes should be ignored. I will respect them."

"Such respect is unusual," she informed him. "It has been our unfortunate experience to interact with people who are curious at best and intrusive at worst. Your forbearance is appreciated."

Stan nodded.

"How long will you stay here?" she asked.

"Until the task is done."

"No longer?"

"No," Stan replied. "I have friends at home who miss me and who I miss in return."

"Ladies?"

"Two of them are," he confirmed. "The other is a young man who is ill. I would be there with them to see that all is well."

They reached the overgrown parking lot, and Stan saw Tom standing there. Miss drifted away, and Stan walked toward Tom.

"Is everything alright?" Stan asked.

Tom shook his head. "I found your name and photo on a couple of sites on the dark web. Posters are saying people should report if they see you. Monetary rewards if it turns out to be a true sighting. That's not a good thing, Stan."

"You are correct, it is not," Stan agreed. "However, I cannot leave before we find out where Ezra Pettigrew is hiding."

"This could end badly for you," Tom remarked.

"I know. There is naught else I can do," Stan reminded him. "Pettigrew needs to be punished for what he did, and I must ensure the safety of the town. When those two things are done, I will return home."

"And if you can't?"

Stan looked at the young man and answered, "Then I will be dead, and I hope I will not care." He sighed and looked out over the field. "I do not wish to return as a ghost."

CHAPTER 12
PERFECT VIEWS

Robert sat in his car with a large map of the town spread out on the seat beside him. He took a bite from his donut, washed it down with some tepid coffee and glanced over his notes.

He and Mr. Pettigrew had spent the better part of the night selecting areas and buildings to put the ghosts in. Not only was placement important, but they had to consider the natural, energy-draining effects of the ghost on any electrical system.

In the end, they had found not only a place for each ghost, but a backup as well. Robert didn't want to be forced to rely on only one location. Getting arrested for trespassing was not ideal.

He finished his coffee and then his donut, instantly regretting the order in which he had done so. The donut sat heavy in his stomach, and he wondered if he should get something else to drink.

He shook his head and forced himself to focus on the task before him.

From the container of haunted items, he selected a black fountain pen and exited the car. He carried it to a small corner store and entered, nodding good morning to the older woman standing behind the register. Robert walked to the back freezer and made a quick glance at the goods. He saw a bottle of chocolate milk, opened the freezer door and slid the fountain pen into a crevice in the rack while retrieving the milk.

The lights in the freezer flickered for a moment, but nothing more happened. Robert smiled, straightened up and closed the door. He carried the milk to the counter, exchanged pleasantries with the woman, and paid cash for the purchase. He slipped the change into his pocket, stepped outside and chuckled.

The task wasn't going to be as difficult as he feared.

✳ ✳ ✳

It wasn't difficult, but it took longer than he had suspected.

Eight hours from start to finish, and Robert felt as though he had run a marathon. He had never realized how large the town really was or how much small talk he was going to have to make. Several of the primary locations had been inaccessible, and so he had been forced to utilize the secondary ones, which had resulted in even more time than originally planned.

Robert opened the door to his car and almost fell into the driver's seat. He was tired to the bone, as his mother had been fond of saying, and he needed to rest, at least for a few minutes, before he returned to the office and faced the barrage of noise from the contractors.

He closed his eyes and considered the ghosts he had placed around the town. Each of them knew their job and what to report when he checked on them, and that, too, would be difficult. It would require continual trips to their locations and distracting anyone else long enough to get the report. Most, Robert assumed, would have nothing to say, but some, he hoped, most certainly would.

He frowned at the idea of gathering the intelligence from the dead. The thought of speaking with them was not only distasteful but, if he was honest with himself, frightening as well.

Robert understood Mr. Pettigrew's use of the dead, and he understood that his employer was, without any doubt, a man who excelled at unique business plans. Robert, however, didn't have to like the finer points of the plan.

He shook his head and corrected himself.

It wasn't a matter of like or dislike. It was simply a matter of fear.

He was afraid.

His entire life, Robert had been afraid of the idea of ghosts. It was why he didn't watch horror movies, didn't read horror stories, and wasn't a fan of Halloween. His wife had been the opposite, but she had never pushed him to embrace those things.

Mr. Pettigrew wasn't forcing him, either; he was asking. Mr. Pettigrew had done a great deal for Robert over the years. In fact, the only reason there had been a funeral and a burial with a headstone had been because of Mr. Pettigrew. He had paid for it all.

Mr. Pettigrew had taken care of Robert during his darkest days, and Robert would never forget it. He would deal with the dead for Mr. Pettigrew. He would, in truth, do whatever the man asked.

Robert put on his seatbelt, started the car and shifted into gear. He needed to get back to the office and report to Mr. Pettigrew.

CHAPTER 13

FINDING THE MARK

"This him?" Gregory asked.

Elliot looked up from his sandwich, squinted and nodded. "Yup. That's the guy."

Gregory put his phone down and finished his soda. "Name's Sam?"

"Stan," Elliot corrected. "Stan Owens."

Gregory shrugged. "We doin' this as a grab job?"

"Was thinkin' that."

"We'll need somebody else," Gregory told him. "If he fights back at all. Kind of looks like he would."

"Think so?" Elliot asked.

"Yeah. I mean, if he was a broad, probably not. Guy, though? We want to make sure there's at least three of us." Gregory glanced out the window of the restaurant. "I think Micky's free."

Elliot groaned and dropped the last bite of his sandwich to his plate. "Really? Micky?"

"I know you don't like him," Gregory said. "But that don't matter. He's big, he's mean, and he can take orders. If this guy Stan can fight at all, we'll need Micky just to get him into the van."

Elliot grunted.

Gregory looked at his partner for a moment and wondered if the last stint in prison had been a little too much for Elliot. He didn't quite have the same edge.

"You up for this?" Gregory asked.

"Huh? Yup, I am. Just don't want to deal with Micky. You didn't do any time with him."

"Come on," Gregory laughed. "You told me you weren't even in the same block as him."

"Wasn't," Elliot muttered. "He stayed neutral, too. That was the problem. Didn't know where he stood."

"Yeah, you did," Gregory corrected. "You just didn't like where he stood. Micky ain't got beef with anybody 'cause of what they look like, just who they run with."

Elliot snorted and looked away.

"Well, lose that attitude," Gregory snapped. "This is a big payoff, and I don't want to miss out on it."

"I was thinkin' about that," Elliot said.

Gregory raised an eyebrow. "Thinkin' about it how?"

"Well, it's a pretty big payday, so why don't we just do the guy when we find him? Be easier to move a body than to carry him out while he's still alive."

"Sure is," Gregory nodded in agreement. "Except if we get stopped, we can't pass a dead guy off as a drunk. We can pass a knocked-out guy as a drunk 'cause if the cops check on him, he's just passed out. If he's dead, then we're going away for the rest of our lives, Elliot. I've done enough time in prison. I don't want to do anymore. Okay?"

Gregory didn't catch what Elliot muttered, but that didn't matter since the man nodded his head in agreement.

"Good," Gregory said. "Let me give Micky a call."

Taking out his phone, Gregory brought up Micky's information and called the man. It rang several times before it was answered.

"Who's this?" Micky's voice, thick and rough, sounded as though it might break the phone.

"Hey, it's Gregory Moat. Heard you were free."

Micky snorted. "For now. Got a broad coming over in a couple of hours, but other than that, nothing's on the schedule. What do you need?"

"Elliot and I are picking up a friend," Gregory told him. "Got a lot of baggage with him."

"You're friend a good tipper?"

"Honestly," Gregory said, "haven't seen a guy who tips this well before."

"Okay, I'll leave the phone on," Micky chuckled. "Call me when he's ready to be picked up."

"Okay."

Gregory ended the call and put the phone down.

Elliot looked at him. "Micky's in?"

"Micky's in," Gregory nodded. "Finish up so we can get out of here. I want to find this guy before anybody else does."

CHAPTER 14
BOSTON MEMORIES

"You sure it was this guy?" Gregory asked.

The woman nodded, sniffed and dragged the back of her hand across her nose. "Yeah, he went into the diner about twenty minutes ago. Hey, you payin' or what? I need to score, and I can't work if I'm talkin' to you."

Gregory glanced at the woman, saw the bags beneath her eyes and the needle tracks up her arm. She'd be dead in a month, if not sooner.

He reached into his pocket and pulled out the five twenties he had put in there before getting out of the car. "Here. Enjoy your ride."

The woman grunted, accepted the money and slipped away down an alley.

"You think she's telling the truth?" Elliot asked.

"Of course I do," Gregory laughed. "She knows I'd beat her if she was lying."

Micky shifted his position against the empty storefront and looked around. "How long have we been waiting for this guy?"

"Long as it takes," Gregory replied. "He's a big payout."

Micky sighed and folded his thick arms over a chest that seemed impossibly broad.

"That's him," Elliot whispered, and the three men looked to the diner's door.

The target, Stan Owens, stepped off to one side of the door, double-checking the buttons on his suit coat.

Gregory looked at Micky, was about to ask if he was ready, and then stopped.

A confused expression settled on Micky's face. He blinked several times, opened his jacket, removed a hard case and extracted a pair of glasses. Gregory would have laughed at the sight of the small frames on the large man's face, but the intense look silenced him.

Micky shook his head, and his skin paled. The large man's hands trembled as he took off his glasses and put them away.

"Don't do this," he stated, his voice shaking and his Boston accent thick. "You don't want any of that guy."

"Him?" Elliot asked, jerking a finger at Owens, who appeared to be having a conversation with the wall of the diner.

"Him," Micky nodded. "He's as bad as they come. You'll need a hell of a lot more than three men to get a hold of him."

"That guy is nothing," Gregory chuckled.

"That's Stan Owens," Micky said, and the fear in his voice sent shivers rippling through Gregory. "I've seen him do things they do in horror movies. I don't know how many people he helped disappear when he was just a teenager. He worked for Old Man Tar out of New Hampshire, and the last person you wanted upset with you or your outfit was the old man. Owens was his muscle."

"He doesn't look like muscle anymore," Elliot remarked.

"He looked even less like it then." Micky shook his head. "I'm out, guys. Nothing is worth getting killed for, and that's what he's going to do. He's going to kill you both. Take it from me, I've seen him at work, and it ain't pretty."

"You're leavin'?" Gregory asked, unable to hide the shock in his voice.

Micky looked at him. "I want to keep livin', Gregory. If you want to do the same, come with me and get a drink. We'll find a different score."

Gregory watched as Micky stepped away from the store and left in the opposite direction Stan was facing.

"Are you serious?" Elliot asked. He turned to face Gregory. "Is he really walkin' away 'cause of this old guy?"

"Guess so," Gregory muttered. A knot of worry formed in his stomach. "Think he's right about it?"

Elliot shook his head. "I bet he's tryin' to scare us."

"Scare us?!" Gregory looked at Elliot. "He looked terrified!"

Elliot snorted. "He's a good actor, that's all. Come on, Gregory. Bet you ten to one he's goin' find someone else to help him grab that mark."

Gregory frowned. "Micky ain't like that."

"Just 'cause he hasn't done it before, don't mean he won't do it now," Elliot stated.

Gregory shifted his attention back to Owens, who was nodding and gesturing. For a moment, Gregory wondered if a cop would pick the man up for being off his rocker.

"Come on," Elliot insisted. "We can do this now. Either way he goes, we can get ahead of him. It'll be easy. Nothin' to worry about."

Owens turned and walked towards them, hands behind his back and his head slightly down as though listening to a conversation.

"We'll duck down on the other side here," Elliot said. "Come back up between Forting & Sons and that new Greek place. It'll be quick. Both of 'em are closed."

Gregory hesitated, then nodded. "Okay."

They hurried along the alley, Elliot leading the way. They reached the second alley and turned down it. As they neared the end, Owens stepped into the opening and faced them.

His hands were no longer behind his back but loose at his sides.

Gregory and Elliot came to a stop, and Gregory held back his surprise.

Owens looked at him and then Elliot before asking, "What do you want with me?"

"A little chat," Elliot answered, taking the lead. "That's all."

"Lying is a bad habit," Owens informed him. He unbuttoned his suitcoat, and Gregory tensed.

Neither he nor Elliot had brought a piece with them. Both had felonies under their belts, and getting caught with a pistol was a sure way to go back to prison for a long, long time.

But Owens didn't reach for a weapon or flash one at them in a threatening manner. He stood and waited.

"You goin' to come with us for that chat?" Elliot asked.

"No." Owens undid the large buckle on his belt, slid it out of its loops and then wrapped it around his wrist several times. Nearly a foot of thick leather hung from his fist, the steel buckle swinging like a pendulum.

"I will tell you once, and once only," Owens continued. "If you attack me, I will defend myself. I have no interest in prisoners. This means I will kill you both."

Gregory looked at Elliot and laughed. The sheer audacity of the statement released all the tension Micky's statements had planted in him.

"Yeah," Gregory grinned, nodding to Elliot. "I think you're right. I think Micky was trying to put one over on us."

"Exactly," Elliot laughed. He shifted his position. "Come on now, Stan. Don't make this any harder than it needs to be."

"You know my name," Owens nodded. "The dead girl said as much. It is a shame, is it not, when you are obvious even unto the dead?"

"Kind of thinkin' that killin' you will be doin' you a favor, too," Gregory replied, pointing at Owens. "Come on, now. Let's get this done with."

"Come then, if you will," Owens responded. "Let us see what it is you think you can do."

Elliot, still laughing, moved forward, and Owens' hand was a blur. Gregory watched Elliot's head snap to the right, blood spraying out and coating the wall.

Elliot turned on one heel as though he was dancing and slammed into the wall. Gregory couldn't take his eyes off his partner, who slid down the rough brick wall and collapsed, limp and lifeless to the ground.

"Unfortunate," Owens stated. "But it was expected. Do you still think you can do this, young man?"

Gregory shoved aside his fear and leaped forward.

The belt whistled through the air for a split second, and then the world exploded around him.

***

Stan squatted down and used a paper napkin from the diner to help him go through the pockets of the two dead men. He found a disposable phone on each of them in addition to iPhones. Stan left the iPhones and took the disposables. He didn't bother with the wallets or anything else.

Straightening up, he looked at the dead teenager sitting on a trashcan, watching him with a smirk.

"They were stupid," she told him.

"You are quite correct in your assessment."

"Why are they looking for you?"

"I intend to find out, but I am assuming it is a man who has caused me a great deal of discomfort and distress." Stan retrieved a wet tissue from a pocket, opened it and carefully cleaned his belt buckle and the leather. With that done, he tucked the trash into a suitcoat pocket before putting his belt back on.

"I thought they would have put up more of a fight," she mused.

"They were amateurs," Stan replied. "If they had not been, they would have stayed out of range and attacked at the same time. Thank you again for your timely warning."

She smiled at him, revealing the hole in her teeth and a glimpse of the brick wall behind her. "You're welcome. Guys like them are the reason why I'm dead."

"I'm sorry."

"Don't be," she said, looking down at her hands. "I was never treated this nice when I was alive."

Stan reached into his pocket, clutched the cold coin in his hand and brought it out. He looked at the penny, a heart-shaped hole punched through its center and asked, "Would you like to return with me, Penny?"

She grinned at him. "You figured out my name."

"I guessed."

"It was a good guess. Yeah, I'd like to," she nodded. "If that's okay."

"I would not have asked if it was not."

"I like you, Stan," Penny told him. "Let's see where you live."

With the phones in his pockets, Stan stepped over the dead men and left them where they lay.

CHAPTER 15
POSITIVE IDENTIFICATION

With the construction and armoring of the building finished, Ezra sat in his office and enjoyed the silence. He looked at his cooling cup of coffee and smiled. The day before, he would have seen ripples in the liquid.

Chuckling, he reached out, took hold of the coffee and brought it to his lips. As he took a sip, a gentle knock sounded on the door.

"Come in," Ezra called.

Robert entered a moment later, a smile on his face while holding a manila envelope.

"Good news?" Ezra asked.

"Yes, sir," Robert confirmed, nodding. He closed the door behind him and went to his accustomed seat. "However, it is not so good for those who delivered the information."

Robert opened the envelope, slid out several photographs and laid them out on the table. The first two images were side profile shots of Stan Owens. The third and fourth pictures were of a pair of men in an alley. They were, without any doubt, dead.

"Two of the men hired by proxy through the Waverly brothers," Robert explained. "They managed to take pictures of Stan in Norwich and sent them to the brothers, who in turn forwarded them to me. Stan killed the men when they tried to take him, and it appears he took their cellphones as well."

"Who took the pictures of them dead?" Ezra asked, gathering the photos together and handing them back to Robert.

He put them away, replying, "Lockwood. Our newest police

acquisition."

Ezra nodded. "See he is sufficiently rewarded, Robert. This is excellent work."

"Of course, sir."

"I want to move on this quickly," Ezra continued. "I want to see Stan Owens' body sooner rather than later."

"Understood, sir."

Ezra took another drink of coffee. "Why do you think he took the phones?"

Robert shook his head. "I don't know. They're burner phones without any way to trace them back to us or anyone else."

"Hmm." Ezra rubbed his chin. "I wonder if he knows that."

"Probably not," Robert smiled. "He probably thinks he can access some information, but even that would be extremely limited if he's skilled enough to do so."

"And if he were to hire a hacker as we have?"

Robert shook his head. "Even a hacker would only be able to pull limited information, sir. Who they were in contact with, and since they were never in contact with us, we needn't be concerned. Even the Waverly brothers haven't used their burner phones to contact us. Those phones are only used for communications between the Waverlys and their proxies."

Ezra nodded, a sense of relief sliding over him. He had worried, perhaps needlessly, that Stan Owens would be clever enough to track them through the phones. But if not even a professional hacker could do such a thing, then his worry was misplaced.

"This is most welcome information, Robert," Ezra informed him and finished his coffee. "You'll reach out to the Waverly brothers, then?"

"I will," Robert said. "We want Stan removed as soon as possible. I'm sure they'll move quickly on it. They haven't disappointed us before, and from what I've heard, they take some pride in their work."

"Good. Very good." Ezra tapped on his coffee mug. "Do they have a way of disposing of him?"

"I'm certain they do, sir," Robert replied. "And I'm certain we shouldn't ask."

"Oh, no, I wouldn't ask," Ezra chuckled. "Sometimes I wonder out loud. No, I'll accept whatever they tell us, so long as there is physical evidence of Stan's untimely demise."

"Understood. I do have another bit of information you might take pleasure in," Robert told him.

Ezra raised an eyebrow.

"Abigail made coffee cake, sir," Robert smiled. "And fresh icing for it as well."

"That sounds amazing," Ezra grinned. "Let us make fresh coffee and enjoy Abigail's cake, which, I am certain, is a triumph."

Laughing, they stood up together, and a warm sense of satisfaction and fulfillment enveloped Ezra.

Stan Owens would soon be dead, and the world would be a better place for it.

CHAPTER 16
WAITING

Tom had the phones, and there was nothing more Stan could do.

He could and did accept that. So, he did what he preferred doing.

He walked.

Stan found himself in Norwich once more, letting his feet guide him. All cities, he had long ago decided, were the same. He knew he could never truly be lost in one. Out of one, traveling along the country roads, yes, he could be lost.

But not in a city. Turned around and confused, but not lost.

As he walked, Stan let his mind wander. He wondered how he had been found in Norwich and if there were others looking for him in the city. Logic dictated the two men who had attacked him were not alone, and thus, his walk served another purpose.

Stan was bait.

He hoped he would not be shot. He knew it to be a gamble that others might be more cautious in their approach despite it being risky regarding any assassin's future freedom.

Stan didn't mind the gamble. The odds were in his favor. Most professionals he had known wouldn't risk a shot in the dark. There was no way to tell if the kill was confirmed, not unless you ran out and checked the body to see if a coup de grace was needed.

No, the next pair that tried to grab him, and he felt certain there would be another attempt, would be better than the first. Stan didn't think it would be easy or pleasant, and that brought a smile to his face.

He was enjoying the violence, so he forced his smile back into the warrens of his mind. He didn't want to smile. Didn't want to look forward to the thrill of beating a man down and killing him.

But it was there, and there was no denying it.

Stan kept walking.

✳ ✳ ✳

Ethan and Hazen looked at Micky, who sat across the small round table from them. A pitcher of beer stood in the center, and each man had a mug. Not much beer remained, and Micky had drunk most of it.

"How do you know him again?" Hazen asked, and Ethan resisted the urge to give his brother a Charley horse.

Micky, as a general rule, didn't like answering questions more than once.

"Boston," Micky replied with a surprising lack of animosity. "I saw that kid, well, man, now, do stuff I don't want to remember."

Hazen glanced at Ethan, who shook his head.

Micky cleared his throat, then poured the rest of the beer into his mug. "Once, we found out that a local priest had robbed a few of the widows in his parish. Scammed 'em, really, but nobody was happy about it. Since he was the parish priest, though, nobody wanted to be the one to deal with him. The job was farmed out to a guy from New Hampshire. Well, he came down with this kid, this Stan Owens. The kid couldn't have been more than fifteen. Hell, I was only twenty myself."

Micky paused and took a drink. "My boss told 'em what had been done and how he wanted the priest punished."

"Not killed?" Ethan asked.

Micky shook his head. "Nope. Just punished. Reminded the guy from New Hampshire that he wanted the priest alive, definitely not dead. Dead would put a serious wrinkly in their business relationship."

Ethan raised his hand and motioned to the bartender, and a minute later, a fresh pitcher replaced the empty. He refilled his and his brother's glasses.

"So, with that squared away," Micky continued, "this guy sent the kid into the church, where the priest had just finished up with Saturday confessions. He came out ten, maybe fifteen minutes later. His hair was wet, and his face was expressionless. That sticks with me, you know. That empty look on his face. The kid walked out, handed up a balled-up cassock to the man, and went to the truck they had driven down in."

"What did he do?" Hazen asked.

Micky snorted, finished the beer in one long gulp and then wiped his mouth with the back of his hand. Ethan poured him another drink, and Micky nodded his thanks.

"We went in," Micky said. "We could hear whimpering coming from one of the confessionals. Donny McGuire opened the door, turned around and puked out his lunch, breakfast and dinner from the night before. I went up and almost lost my lunch, too, if I hadn't kept my mouth shut. The priest was in there, and his left hand was on the floor. His right arm was suspended above him, and he'd been skinned from the wrist to the elbow. It hung in long strips that reminded me of red streamers."

Hazen swore, and Micky nodded.

"I saw some other work he did, too," Micky added. "It was always like that. Always something you would never expect some normal, sane person would do. Kept people afraid. Kept 'em all honest."

Ethan rubbed his face with both hands, dropped them to his lap and asked, "This really happened?"

Micky let out a bitter chuckle. "More than once. Lots more."

"Cops never picked him up?" Ethan asked.

"Some were paid to look the other way. The others didn't care. The kid was hurting bad guys, you know?"

"And the ones who did care?" Ethan said.

"They stopped caring."

"Why?" Hazen asked.

"I know nobody knows about this," Micky said, looking down at the empty mug in his hands. "But there was a guy who messed around with kids. Did bad things. Hurt them. Well, Stan Owens, he found out about it and came down to Boston on his own. Cops had the guy in a safe house so nobody would kill him before trial. Owens went in, took the guy out."

"Without the cops knowing?" Ethan asked.

Micky nodded. "We thought maybe he had paid off one or two, but he hadn't. He couldn't have paid enough, not with a high-profile case like that one. No, he got in there on his own, although nobody figured out how he did it. Or how he even found the safe house. But he found it, he stole the guy away. Cops found him two weeks later after Owens called and told them where the remains were."

"Must have smelled terrible," Hazen offered up.

Micky looked at him and shook his head. "No. He'd only been dead a few hours, close as they could tell. 'Course, most of him was scattered around the building they found him in."

Ethan frowned. "Are you saying he chopped him up and spread him about before calling the cops?"

"I'm saying he tortured him for two weeks." Micky's voice had sunk low. "His torso and head were intact. For the most part. The rest of him, well, the cops said Owens had cut him apart day by day until he finally died."

"I'm gonna puke," Hazen mumbled and left the table.

Ethan's own stomach twisted and turned. He'd done some bad things in the past. More than a few beat downs and the occasional killing, but torture like that? No. Not at all. Guys might be missing a few teeth and have a couple of broken bones, but that was about it.

"I told them to leave him alone," Micky stated, and he poured the last of the beer from the pitcher into his mug.

"I know you did," Ethan replied. "Thing is, somebody wants him bad,

Micky."

"Well, make sure whoever it is has a lot of money," Micky said, taking a drink.

"Why's that?"

"'Cause he's gonna have to pay for a lot of funerals."

CHAPTER 17
OWENS IN THE WILD

"You think Micky's telling the truth?" Hazen asked.

"Why would he lie, is the better question."

Hazen frowned.

"Listen," Ethan sighed. "Micky's not trying to get us away from the target, right?"

Hazen nodded.

"Not only that, he's absolutely hammered," Ethan continued. "He couldn't go after Owens even if he wanted to. And, I don't know if you noticed, but Micky's scared out of his mind. When he talks about Stan Owens, it's like he's five and talking about the boogeyman. Nah, he's not lying to us, and he's got no reason to."

"I guess that makes it a little tougher then," Hazen grumbled.

"Oh yeah?"

Hazen frowned. "Yeah. If we get too close to him, he's gonna fight. You saw the pictures. Those boys were beaten down. Not bad, but enough to kill 'em."

"Yeah," Ethan agreed. "Talked to Pat at the coroner's office. Guess it was just a couple of hits, the docs are thinking that maybe he had a blackjack or something like that, but with sharp edges. Anyway, he's definitely dangerous up close."

"Guns are out of the question," Hazen continued. "We get caught with 'em, and we're done."

"We're gonna have to jump him, whether we want to or not."

Hazen groaned. "We still want to do this alone?"

Ethan nodded. "Too many people make it a mess. Just the two of us can do it together, or it can't be done at all."

"Yeah. That's true."

"So," Ethan looked at his brother. "You ready to find him and grab him?"

"As long as we're about to finish him off and not waiting around or anything."

"That's the plan. Kill him, collect the bounty and get the hell out of here for a while," Ethan assured him.

"Okay. Let's find him."

Owens enjoyed Norwich.

It was a small city, and the roads were comforting in their likeness to other cities he had walked in. Names were nearly identical. Streets such as Elm and Pine, Ash and Oak, Washington and Broad. The streets were narrow and twisting, the houses old and crowding the curbs. Buildings of red brick stood tall above him in the night, and old sodium lights cast their yellow glow down onto the city streets.

Soon, he knew, they would find him again, and the dead would warn him.

The dead watched from various places, amused at his wanderings and pleased with his conversations. He did not force his company upon them but was more than amicable to pausing for a chat.

A young man, dressed for running and with his chest caved in from an unfortunate incident with a truck ten years earlier, appeared from a building.

"Someone's coming," the ghost told Stan. "Two men. There's a small shed behind the building across from you."

Stan nodded his thanks, crossed the road and made his way to a shed that was older than him. The door was propped open, and Stan slid inside and waited.

Within a few minutes, a pair of men passed by the building, and Stan knew them for what they were. Hired thugs, killers if need be. Men who knew what they were about, a fact driven home by the calm, collected way they moved.

They were looking for him, and they didn't look out of place despite the late hour. Being stopped by the police wouldn't trigger any warnings from an investigating officer. Stan doubted the men were armed, but he did not doubt they lacked the ability to kill him.

When they passed fully by the building, Stan left the shed and made his way back to the street. He saw the men walking ahead of him, and he followed.

Ethan glanced over his shoulder and stopped.

Hazen took another step before realizing his brother wasn't beside him. "What is it?"

"Look," Ethan pointed.

Hazen did so, and a moment later, he muttered, "Is that Owens?"

Half a block behind them, Stan Owens walked toward them.

Ethan knew it wasn't a matter of Owens traveling in the same direction, but it was, in fact, Owens walking toward them. Somehow, the man knew they were looking for him.

"This isn't right," Hazen shook his head. "This isn't right at all. We're supposed to be getting him. Not the other way around."

"Doesn't matter how it was supposed to be," Ethan snapped. "All that matters is how it is right now."

Stan Owens came to a stop at the mouth of a narrow alley. He nodded at Ethan and Hazen, turned left and walked down the alley.

Neither of the brothers hesitated.

Ethan went first and saw Owens had almost reached the far end. The man didn't turn to either side but continued into a large yard. By the time the brothers stepped into the yard, Owens had come to a stop at a low, abandoned building. Most of the windows were boarded up, and Owens stood at a door. He nodded once, twisted the doorknob and forced his way in.

Owens didn't close the door. He walked into the darkness.

"He's trapping himself," Hazen chuckled, and Ethan grinned.

Owens might be a dangerous guy in a fight, but he was a fool in every other sense. In a confined space, he and Hazen could take anyone.

They entered the building, and Hazen tried a light switch. A weak, faded light illuminated the hall, revealing footprints in the dust. The tracks passed four doors and then exited through the door at the other end of the hallway.

A door that was closed.

The fight would be there, in whatever room was beyond the warped wood. Owens would fight, and he would fight well. But Ethan and Hazen would win, and they would smother him or strangle him, whichever was easier.

They had done it before, and they would do it again.

The men approached the door.

CHAPTER 18
IN THE BUILDING

The room was as promised.

Large and empty.

There were no windows and only a single other door directly across from the first. The lights flickered, their wan glow illuminating the center of the room but leaving the corners hidden. The dead had told him of the room and told him of how it might be used if he so chose.

In a moment, the door across from him would open, and the men would enter.

Stan took off his coat, folded it and set it on the floor. Slowly, meticulously, he rolled up his sleeves. As the doorknob twisted and the door opened, he slipped his belt out of the loops, wrapped the excess leather around his hand and waited.

Ethan closed the door and stepped to the right as Hazen moved off to the left. Stan Owens stood in the center of the room, his belt hanging from his hand, the heavy buckle swinging freely.

No blackjack, Ethan realized. Just someone who had been taught how to fight.

That thought reminded him of the warnings issued by Micky.

They were going to have to be careful. Far more careful than they had ever been.

Owens' face was unreadable, his eyes shifting from Ethan to Hazen and back again.

"My name is Stan Owens," he said into the stillness. "I know you have come to kill me. You are not the first to try, and you will not be the last. I will ask you to consider whether the price on my head is worth your life. I will ask that you consider leaving your phones with me so I might track down the person who hired you."

Neither Ethan nor Hazen responded, and Owens nodded.

"Come then," he said. "Let's be done with it."

Hazen moved in first, his eyes on Owens while Ethan stepped around to the side. His heart thumped as he waited for an opening, a chance to see where the man might shift to. Hazen sprang forward, launching a quick jab at Owens' face.

Owens shifted a fraction of an inch, the punch missing as he snapped the belt out toward Hazen's face.

The metal buckle glanced off Hazen's ear as he twisted away. Blood sprayed from the cut, and Ethan dashed in, preparing to deliver a punch to the back of Stan's head.

But Stan shifted his weight and dropped low, Ethan's blow going over him. Ethan gasped as a fist smashed into his rib cage, lifting him off his feet and sending him stumbling back. He remained out of striking range, and he and Hazen kept Owens between them.

Stan Owens let the belt hang freely, and he looked placidly from Hazen to Ethan.

It was then that Ethan understood a calculated attack wouldn't work. Not on Stan. Their best bet would be to overwhelm him, to get in close where any of his skills would be useless to him. Ethan looked at Hazen, saw in his brother's expression that he had come to the same conclusion, and then looked at Stan.

Owens stood and waited.

So, the brothers sprinted toward him.

CHAPTER 19
COLLECTION BUILDING

The men knew how to fight.

Their blows, those that landed, were well-aimed and hard-hitting. They struck for the main muscle groups, seeking to deaden them. Fingers and thumbs sought out eyes, and knees tried to slam into Stan's groin. Fists landed against kidneys and sought the softness of his stomach.

Cuts opened above his eyes, and blood seeped down over his face.

Stan did not attempt to wipe his face. When the blood covered his eyes, he blinked it away. He didn't need to see the men to fight them. Their goal was to get in close enough to achieve control, and so they were always near enough to strike.

One man grunted as he grabbed hold of Stan's right wrist, and Stan, in turn, took hold of the man's pinky and snapped the bone, forcing the man to let go.

The other came in close, and Stan managed to bring the buckle up in a sharp arc, striking the man under the chin. Teeth clacked together with enough force to chip them, and the man staggered back, spitting out shards.

The man with the broken finger swore and barreled forward, all sense of restraint and skill gone.

It was what Stan had been waiting for, and he let his own anger, guided by the cold brutality instilled in him by his granduncle, flow from him.

Stan let the broken-fingered man hit him, bracing his stomach as the man struck. With his left fist, Stan smashed it into the man's thick neck. The attacker paused, gasped, and sank to his knees. Taking a step back,

Stan swung, and the buckle whistled in the air before colliding with the man's temple. A crack rang out, and the attacker dropped to the floor, limp and unmoving.

The second man hesitated for a moment, then howled, his face a mask of mixed rage and disbelief. Incoherent words exploded from his mouth, and he swung wildly at Stan as he moved forward.

Stan kept out of range, recognizing the power in each fist, knowing the fury-driven blows would be difficult to recover from.

Yet with each wild swing, Stan lashed out with the belt.

Again and again the buckle struck the man's head, sometimes fully, other times only glancing blows. Yet each drew blood. The enraged man tried to lift his head to get a better look at Stan, and the buckle caught his right eye with enough force to break the orbital bone and force the eye to close and swell up.

The man gasped, tried to shift his position and ended up stumbling over the first man's body. As the half-blinded man crashed toward the floor, Stan hit him again with the buckle, the metal striking the forehead with enough force to leave an imprint.

The stranger slumped onto the floor and lay beside his companion.

Stan stood panting, heart racing.

The lights dimmed, and the dead man with the crushed chest peered in through a wall. "Did you kill them?"

Stan looked down at the men. "Not yet."

"Oh." The ghost looked around. "No chance of letting them live?"

"No. No chance at all," Stan told him.

"Guess that makes sense," the ghost remarked. Then, with a smile, he added, "We were watching the whole time. It was one heck of a fight, Stan."

Stan felt the dull throb of injuries seeping through his adrenaline and nodded his head in agreement. "Yes, it most certainly was."

The ghost laughed and then vanished.

Stan got down on his knees and searched the men. He found four phones. Two of them were identical to the two he had taken from the previous men. He slid those into his back pockets and looked at the men on the floor.

Stan had no doubt they had been sent to kill him, just as he had no doubt they would try should they recover from this fight.

And so, they would not recover.

With a grimace, Stan reached out to the man with the broken finger, pinched his nose and covered his mouth. It wouldn't take long, but there were things Stan needed to do, and killing, even when necessary, was rarely pleasant.

CHAPTER 20
COFFEE AND BISCOTTI

Tom enjoyed the Liberty Coffee Shop more than any other. Perhaps more than he should. But they made the best biscotti he had ever tasted, and so he allowed himself the small vice of visiting on a regular basis.

Entering the shop, Tom waved at the owner, Diana, and made his way to his preferred seat at the coffee bar. In a moment, Diana brought over a plate with three large biscotti coated in chocolate and a black coffee.

"How are you?" she asked.

"Well enough," Tom answered.

"Check on your dad lately?"

Tom nodded. "The other day. He's the same as when I left him."

"That's not going to change, Tom."

"I know." He offered a tired smile. "I'm about as okay as I can be with that fact. Still, I hope something can get better. Maybe if just a little bit comes back to him before he goes."

"I know your dad," Diana told him, her voice gentle. "I don't think it would do him any good to have even a hint of what's going on with himself."

"You're right."

"I may be right, but it doesn't mean it's not terrible," she said, rapping her knuckles on the counter for added emphasis. "Anyway, drink your coffee, eat your biscotti."

"Will do."

Tom picked up one of the biscotti and dipped it into his coffee, letting the liquid soften the bread. After a moment, he took a bite, the chocolate warm and the bread easy to chew.

He took his time, not thinking about Victor, not thinking about school. Thoughts of Stan's issues and the problem with the cell phones tried to creep up, but he set those aside as well. It was time to relax, at least for a short while, and that's what he intended to do.

By the time he finished the second biscotti, he had gone through a second cup of coffee as well, and as he waited to catch Diana's attention, the chime above the door went off, announcing the arrival of a new customer. Tom looked over and caught sight of a young woman entering, and a warm flush went up his neck, settled in his cheeks and caused him to swallow once.

The young woman wore tight jean shorts that ended just above her thighs and black leggings that went down into well-worn Doc Marten boots. A baggy black sweatshirt, absent of any sort of decoration, covered her upper body, and her short, crewcut hair was dyed a deep purple. She glanced at Tom and flashed a smile, the light of the shop catching in her various piercings. In one hand she carried a book, which she set down on the counter as she took a seat only a few from Tom.

He listened as Diana went over and took the young woman's order.

Black with three biscotti.

"You might as well be his twin," Diana said, gesturing toward Tom as she wrote down the order. "Right down to the reading material."

Tom straightened up, and the young woman looked at him with a broad smile.

"What are you reading?" she asked.

"I'm rereading Steinbeck's *Cannery Row*," he told her, and she laughed as she held up her book.

"I'm rereading *Tortilla Flat*."

Tom grinned. "Would you like some company?"

"I would," she nodded.

Tom slid his empty cup and biscotti plate over two seats, settled down and introduced himself.

"I'm Lisbeth," she replied, shaking his hand. "It's a pleasure to meet you."

"Likewise," Tom responded.

Diana walked over, topped off Tom's coffee and gave Lisbeth her order. And as she did so, Tom and Lisbeth began to talk.

✳ ✳ ✳

They stood outside together in the early afternoon sun. They had talked for hours, and Tom felt as though he could talk for hours more. He looked at Lisbeth and she blushed, and then he did the same.

He let out a laugh and shook his head. "You're fantastic, Lisbeth."

She punched him playfully in his prosthetic arm, grinning at the thunk of her knuckles against it. "You, too. So, you have classes tonight?"

Tom nodded. "What are you up to?"

"I've got some books I'm looking to buy for my sister," she answered. "Private dealer. You have my number. You want to shoot me a text when you finish and maybe grab a drink?"

"I would love that. It's been a long time since I just relaxed."

She frowned, then said, "You'll have to tell me why tonight."

"Sounds good to me."

"Too soon for a hug?" she asked.

He shook his head and embraced her. The press of her body against him felt not just perfect but absolutely right. The smell of her, sweet and harsh at the same time, enveloped him, and he was only slightly surprised when she lifted her head up and kissed him.

It was a quick kiss, nothing aggressive.

But it was beautiful.

He looked into her eyes, hazel and sharp, and grinned. "Thank you."

"You're welcome." She kissed him quickly on the nose. "That's why

I kissed you. Because I knew you would say thank you. You're special, Tom. I can't explain it."

He nodded. "I feel the same."

"Good."

She stepped out of his embrace. "Text me soon?"

"Definitely."

She waved, turned and walked away, glancing once over her shoulder to blow him another kiss.

When she had turned the corner, Tom let out a deep breath and tried to clear his thoughts. He was, he realized, going to have a difficult time focusing on his schoolwork.

But that wasn't a terrible thing. It had been a long time since he could focus on anything other than work, his father, or anything other than himself.

Now, though, there was Lisbeth, and she liked him.

Tom started towards the library, where he had several books waiting, and wondered what she might think of the books at his home.

CHAPTER 21
UNWANTED INFORMATION

Ezra woke up with a headache, and his day went quickly downhill.

He managed, without any real effort, to set the water for his shower to hot and seared himself fully awake.

His favorite shirt, and he couldn't believe he still had such a thing, tore at the underarm all the way down the seam when he put it on. When he went to slide his belt through the loops of his trousers, it slipped, and the buckle swung down and smashed against his knee. Had he any neighbors, they most certainly would have been surprised by the broad selection of profanity that he used.

The kitchen went no better.

His coffee maker, which was no more than a few months old, sparked once and then died. The stench of burnt electronics and unused coffee grounds hung in the air. His bagel, the last in the bag, had a spot of fuzz that reminded him of a bit of gray fur. The egg he tried to make in its place filled the kitchen with the odor of brimstone and informed him that the remnants of the dozen were bad.

Escaping his home didn't improve the day, either.

When he climbed into the car and started it, the low tire pressure gauge went off, and Ezra discovered he had no idea where any gas stations with operable air systems were located. Halfway to the office, his engine began emitting a curious ticking sound, and by the time he pulled into his parking space, the tick had turned into a knock.

Ezra turned off the engine and sat in his seat for a moment, gathering his thoughts and focusing them on the day ahead. He would review any information from the ghost sentinels. Hopefully, he would also receive good news from the Waverly brothers or at least about one of the operatives they had put in place.

With a sigh, he exited his car, locked it and made his way into the office building. He nodded good morning to the new security guard who sat by the main entrance and rode the elevator up. When he entered his office, Robert looked up from the coffee maker, where a large pot had just finished brewing.

Ezra smiled and nodded his thanks as Robert poured him a mug.

Wrapping his hands around the warming ceramic, Ezra closed his eyes and inhaled.

"Difficult morning, sir?"

Ezra nodded, then opened his eyes. "Very much so, I'm afraid. Little things, overall, but tiresome. We'll need to find a reputable garage to pick up my car. Something's going on with it, and I'd rather not try and drive it home. It may be nothing, but considering how the day began, I'd rather not test that theory."

"I'll look into it shortly," Robert assured him.

"And how was your morning?" Ezra asked, taking a sip of the coffee.

"Uneventful."

"Always preferable to exciting, let me assure you," Ezra stated. "We will be receiving information from the Waverlys today, correct?"

"Yes," Robert confirmed. He glanced at his watch. "In fact, they should be calling within the next half hour or so."

"Good," Ezra sighed. "Maybe this day can continue in the proper direction. The coffee helps, of course."

Robert chuckled, and Ezra went into his office. He puttered about the room, opening the few blinds on the windows to let in the morning light and powering up his laptop. As he sat down in his chair and made himself comfortable, a gentle knock on the door caught his attention.

"Come in."

The door opened, and Abigail entered, still wearing her coat and scarf. In her hand, she carried a Rubbermaid container. "Robert told me you had a rough start to your day, sir."

"He is correct," Ezra nodded.

"Well, it's a good thing I did some baking this morning," she replied and opened the container when she stopped beside his desk. The sweet smell of fresh cinnamon muffins wafted out and caused his stomach to rumble.

"You are amazing, Abigail," Ezra told her.

She smiled her thanks and handed him one of the muffins. "Do you want me to fetch you a plate and napkin?"

He shook his head. "No need, I have tissues in a drawer, I'll set one of them down beneath it."

"Two," she corrected and took out a second muffin as he retrieved a tissue from the box in the desk drawer. "You need to eat."

"I'm not a growing boy," he chuckled, watching as she set the muffin down.

"No, you've grown into a man."

"Are you fattening me up, Abigail?" he asked with a wink, and the woman blushed.

She wagged a finger at him, closed the lid to the container and left the room. Ezra took a bite of the muffin and savored the taste. Abigail was an exceptional cook, and he never ceased to be amazed at what she would bake before coming to work in the mornings.

In a short time, he had finished both muffins and the cup of coffee. When he stood up to refill his mug, he wondered why the Waverlys hadn't contacted Robert. Or, if they had, why Robert hadn't come and spoken to him.

The Waverlys were punctual and professional. That's what made it such a pleasure dealing with them.

Ezra exited his office and walked to the coffee pot. As he filled his mug, he smiled at Abigail as she worked at her computer. He glanced around, looking for Robert, but the man wasn't in the room.

Ezra frowned, and Abigail pointed to the main entrance.

He opened the door into the broad hallway and saw Robert standing by a window at the far end of the hall. Ezra's frown deepened, and he walked towards the man. Robert's head was bent and slightly angled toward the window, and it took only a heartbeat to realize he was trying to keep a connection with someone on the phone.

"Yes. Yes, understood. Let me know when you do," Robert stated and then straightened up, ending the call as he did so.

"What's wrong?" Ezra asked, disliking Robert's grim expression.

"The Waverlys are dead, sir."

"Was there an accident?"

Robert shook his head. "No. It seems as though we've underestimated Stan Owens. And so did the Waverly brothers. We should be getting photos and possibly video footage of the fight, but that will be a while. The local police are in an uproar. Four homicides in such a short time span is unusual, and it will put the population on edge."

Ezra refrained from making any unnecessary remarks about how little he cared about the local police or the population.

He cleared his throat and asked, "Why were you out here on the call?"

"Reception in the office isn't very good. We'll need a booster of some sort, sir," Robert explained. "The additional reinforcement of the building and the strengthening of the electrical system seems to cause interference with the cellphones."

"We'll get boosters," Ezra stated. "This is absurd."

"I know, sir."

Ezra took a sip of coffee. "There are nine left?"

"Five, sir."

"What?" Ezra asked.

"Four dropped out of the contract when they learned of the Waverlys.

Big Mike has also informed me that he spoke with a man named Micky from South Boston who seems to know Owens," Robert continued. "Micky has attempted to convince him that Owens will be the death of anyone who goes against him."

"I'd like to speak to Micky," Ezra stated after a moment.

"I'll see what I can do about getting him here, sir."

Ezra shook his head. "It doesn't have to be here. Wherever will be fine. I just want to know what he does about Stan Owens. Be sure to offer him a large enough incentive to make talking worth his while."

Robert nodded. "I will, sir."

"Thank you. I'll be in my office. Please let me know when the images and footage are ready. I want to know what we're up against with Owens. I don't want to underestimate him again."

"Of course."

Ezra took another sip, sighed, and then went back. He had an idea itching at the back of his head, and he needed to see if it might work.

CHAPTER 22
RAY

Stan didn't go into Norwich in the evening.

He didn't want to kill anyone else.

But that wasn't true. Not completely. The problem was that he wanted to kill someone else, and he knew he shouldn't. He should leave them alone, even if they were looking for him. All he could do was hope that if any were still looking for him, they would learn of the newest deaths and change their minds.

Until then, maybe the cell phones he had gathered would help Tom.

So, instead of wandering Norwich, Stan walked a country road.

The trees had long since arched up and over the battered asphalt and formed a living tunnel. A handful of streetlights lined the road, but only one of them worked. The others had long since gone out, and he doubted anyone would come out to replace them. Tom lived in a forgotten part of the world, it seemed, and Stan enjoyed it. He preferred to be home in Mason, but this place pleased him.

Stan estimated he was close to five miles from Tom's, and should he go much further, it might be best to settle down off the road for a brief nap before attempting the return trip. His thoughts cleared when a figure stepped out onto the road ahead of him. Streetlight drifted through the figure's shape, and as Stan drew closer, he could make out finer details.

The figure was a man, one dressed in a black and white flannel shirt, jeans and a pair of black boots. His dark hair, thinning on top, was neatly trimmed, as was his gray and white beard, which reached to his chest. The stranger wore glasses, and as he turned to face him, Stan could see a large blood stain on the man's left breast.

As Stan and the dead man looked at one another, the ghost removed his glasses, used a bit of his flannel shirt to polish the lenses, and then replaced them on his nose. Stan wondered if the act, surely done from memory, actually helped with any sort of improvement with the ghost's sight.

"You can see me," the ghost remarked, his deep voice rolling over the ground.

"I can," Stan answered. He came to a stop some fifteen feet from the body.

"Is that a good thing or a bad thing?" the dead man asked.

"It is neither until someone makes it one or the other."

"I like that answer," the dead man smiled. "Name's Ray. Ray King."

"I am Stan Owens."

"A pleasure to meet you, Stan." Ray looked around. "You see ghosts a lot?"

"Yes."

"Well, I don't see people a lot. At least not walking over here. Not only that, fewer ones I see can see me," Ray continued. "Not that that's a bad thing. Not at all. Every so often, there'll be someone who can sense me. Rarest still is the person who can see me. And you're one of those rare ones. You live nearby?"

Stan shook his head. "I am visiting a friend."

"That's nice," Ray remarked. "I haven't visited anyone in, oh, I don't know, about thirty years. I think. It's hard to keep track of time."

"Why are you out here?" Stan asked.

"I was taking a walk," Ray answered, his tone sour. "I went into the woods to go to the bathroom, and I got shot. Some damned fool hunter thought I was a deer and let off a shot. He found me, panicked, and left me behind. There wasn't much he could have done anyway. What would have been a terrible shot at a deer was a great one for me. No suffering.

Can't ask for much more than that."

Ray paused, slipped his hands into his pockets and then added, "'Course, I would have appreciated being buried next to my father, but the woods aren't too bad. Or rather, they aren't now."

Stan waited for Ray to explain.

"Animals," Ray said after a moment. "When I first died, and that hunter had put me in a shallow grave, the animals found me. They pulled me apart. I mean, yeah, I get it. That's what they do, but I wish they hadn't. My bones were scattered just about everywhere you could think of."

"Did no one come to try and find you?"

Ray nodded. "Sure, but the road's long, and there's a lot of woods to look through. They checked the sides of the road but not too far in. And I was pretty far in. I didn't want anyone to accidentally see me going to the bathroom while they were driving by. The hunter, well, he didn't want anyone to figure out what he'd done, so he pulled me even farther in. So, yeah, they looked for me, but they didn't find me. The animals didn't help. When they pulled me apart, they dragged the different parts deeper, too. Everything was against me, and it didn't help that nobody really needed to find me. You know?"

"I do," Stan assured him. "How is it you are close to the road if you were so far from it?"

"That's a good question," the dead man grinned. "Come on, I'll show you."

Stan followed the ghost back into the woods, picking his way through the darkness until Ray said, "Here."

In a pale bit of light that had filtered down to the forest floor, something glittered.

Stan squatted down and saw the remains of a large nest. In the remnants was a silver medallion.

"This is yours," Stan stated and picked up the medallion.

"It is," Ray nodded. "That's my Saint Ignatius medal. It was always important to me. I just didn't realize how important until it was brought here, and so was I."

Stan straightened up and held the worn medal in the palm of his hand. He looked at Ray. "You have been here a long time."

"Yup."

"Would you like to leave?" Stan asked.

Ray looked at him with a confused expression. "What? With you?"

Stan nodded. "I do not go far. Usually. But if you wish to accompany me, I would be happy to bring you."

Ray grinned. "Hell, that sounds like a fantastic idea. Honestly, I never thought of going much farther than wherever the medal ended up. How are you going to carry me?"

"I will put you in my wallet," Stan informed him. "Your medal will be too cold for me to wear."

"And that would be kind of weird if you were wearing it," Ray stated. "I mean, it would be really weird."

"So, you are amicable to the idea?" Stan asked.

"I'd shake your hand if I could," Ray laughed. "But yeah, I'm amicable to the idea."

Stan took out his wallet, put the medal into a small, secure pouch, and then returned the wallet to his pants. "I will walk back to my friend's home if you would care to tell me a little of your story."

"Sounds good to me," Ray replied. "It's been a long, long time since I had anyone to talk to."

"I will listen, Ray," Stan stated. "I have been told it is something I am good at."

Ray laughed and began to talk.

CHAPTER 23
GWEN AND A CALL

"You look tired," Gwen frowned.

"I am," Stan admitted.

"Are you sleeping enough?"

Stan considered the question. "I sleep an average of four and a half hours a night. This is not enough, but it is all I am able to get at this time."

She shook her head. "There's a type of tea I'd like you to find. Ask your friend Tom to help you, okay?"

"Yes."

"The tea is called Sleepy Buddha Tea," she said and paused as he wrote it down in his small notebook. "It's made by Buddha Teas."

Stan nodded and added that information as well.

He looked up when he finished and found her smiling at him. Warmth filled him, and a nervous smile crept onto his face. "What is it, Gwen?"

"You. Just you, Stan," she answered. "I've told other adults, men and women, about this drink, and they've all fought me on it. Just because of the name."

"That is strange."

She shook her head. "The name makes them think I'm treating them like children."

He frowned. "You are a professional, Gwen. They have hired you to help them. Why would they then not listen to your advice?"

"You really are just fantastic, Stan Owens," she grinned. "Don't worry about it. Just know I'm very happy you'll look for the tea."

"Of course."

"So, you're not sleeping enough. Are you eating properly and drinking water?" she asked.

He nodded. "I am most assuredly eating enough. Three meals a day, although it is difficult to be away from the Mason Diner. I drink a great deal of water. I must be alert."

Gwen tilted her head slightly. "Are you being safe, Stan?"

"I am being as safe as I can be," he answered. "At times, there is a fair amount of danger, but I do feel as though I can continue with my search."

She opened her mouth to say something, then closed it. After a moment, she nodded. "Okay. But I want you to make sure you're careful, Stan. I want you to come home. I want to walk with you in Milford. I want to sit with you by the water. We can't do those things if you're hurt."

"I will make certain I am not hurt," he assured her, "because I want those things with you, too."

"Good." She yawned and settled back on her couch, pulling a blanket up around her shoulders. "Tell me, what have you been doing?"

Stan hesitated, considered what to say, and then answered. "I met a ghost named Ray."

Gwen smiled. "And how did you meet him?"

Stan returned the smile and told her.

Morrigan paced her office, worried. She had the distinct suspicion that Pettigrew was going to try and usurp control of the dead she had sent to him. It wouldn't be surprising if he tried to get them to be something other than what they were, and she was worried he might damage those who didn't do as they were told.

Her phone rang, and Morrigan crossed the room to her desk. On the third ring, she answered the phone.

"Morrigan."

"Hey, Sis," Lisbeth greeted.

Morrigan sat in her chair. "Hey, yourself. How are things going down there, any luck?"

"Little bit," Lisbeth stated. "I met up with that dealer and purchased a couple of books off him. No one too violent, though. One's just a little girl, kind of scared about what's going on. I ran into someone, though."

"Who?"

"Does the name Tom Daniels ring any bells?"

Morrigan frowned. "There was a Daniels who took over a large collection a couple of years ago. I don't think his name was Tom, though."

"You're right. His name is Victor, Victor Daniels. Tom is his son, and Tom has control of the collection now. Evidently, something happened to his father." Lisbeth paused. "Tom's young."

"How young?"

"My age," Lisbeth answered.

"How do you know all this?" Morrigan asked.

"I met him in a coffee shop in Norwich," her sister laughed. "We're both reading Steinbeck novels right now and we just started to talk."

Morrigan smiled. "Is he nice?"

"Very," Lisbeth replied, and Morrigan heard a shift in her sister's voice.

"When are you meeting him again?"

"Tomorrow afternoon," Lisbeth answered. "I saw him this evening for a bit. He just left, in fact. That's why the call was so late. I'm sorry."

"Don't be," Morrigan laughed. "I was working on some stuff here in the office. Do you know how much Tom might have in his collection?"

"No idea, but I'm sure I'll find out at some point. I just don't want to pitch anything at him, not right away." Lisbeth cleared her throat. "I like him. I like him a lot."

"You don't have to pitch him anything at all," Morrigan told her. "If it comes up down the road, then fine. Otherwise, don't worry about it.

There are still plenty of ways to source our goods, okay?"

"Okay," Lisbeth sighed. "Any word from Ezra Pettigrew."

"Nothing," Morrigan said. "And I don't know if that's a good or a bad thing."

"Well, let's follow the adage that no news is good news."

Morrigan chuckled. "Yes, I think you're right about that. How long are you going to stay down there?"

"At least another week," Lisbeth told her. "Longer if things work out between Tom and me."

Morrigan raised an eyebrow. "You like him that much?"

"Honestly, sis, I don't think I've ever liked anyone this much. It's strange."

"Don't worry about it, or you're apt to ruin it," Morrigan warned.

"I won't," Lisbeth laughed. "Anyway, I've packaged the books, and I'm sending them up to you. They're on their way and should get in by tomorrow."

"Okay, give me a call tomorrow. Let me know how things worked out with Tom."

Lisbeth agreed, and Morrigan ended the call. She sat in the silence of her small office and looked at the table. After a moment, she picked up her pen, pulled a notepad closer and began to jot down ideas and concerns.

None of them involved Lisbeth or Tom.

Everything, however, revolved around Ezra Pettigrew.

CHAPTER 24

SPIRITUAL TRANSFORMATIONS

Ezra stepped off the small chartered plane feeling better than he had in months. He slung the strap of his satchel over his shoulder and crossed the tarmac toward the rental car waiting for him. The vehicle was a Volkswagen Tiguan, an older model but one suited to the driving he was going to do over the next three days.

Ezra climbed in, pulled down the driver's side visor and caught the keys that dropped down. The paper copy of the rental agreement would be in the glove compartment, as would the basic information he needed regarding available buildings in the area. He didn't need anything extravagant. He only needed something private.

Starting the car, Ezra smiled at the full gas tank and then removed the property information from the glove compartment. He glanced through them quickly, then punched the address into his phone, waiting another minute for it to load up. Once the map was available, he shifted into drive, pulled out of the parking lot and let the voice on the phone guide him.

It took Ezra nearly forty-five minutes to reach the first property, and he immediately discounted it. The building was in the line of sight of several other structures, all of which were currently occupied.

He took out a pen, crossed the first one off the list, and then continued on.

By one in the afternoon, Ezra had gone through the entire list and narrowed his choices down to two. He would need to see the areas they were in after dark. He wanted to make certain there wasn't anything going around in the evening that would compromise him during the day. His new business model was less than orthodox, and he would need his privacy.

Until then, however, he would need food and to check into the hotel, which was another half-hour drive away from the last of the buildings.

When he finally reached his lodgings for the evening, he was not in the best of moods and checked in as quickly as he could. The room didn't help his mood. It was smaller than he was used to, and he disliked the lingering odor of cleaning products that hung in the air.

He shook his head and dropped down into a chair set by the room's solitary window.

He was, he realized, in a decidedly foul mood, and he needed to extract himself from it.

Ezra took out his cell phone and checked his emails. Only one of importance, and that was from Robert.

The email labeled *Updates* had a single sentence in the message portion.

Please, call me, sir.

With a frown, Ezra did so.

Robert answered on the first ring. "Mr. Pettigrew, I have excellent news. Your construction businesses in Southern California sold for twice what you were asking."

Ezra blinked and then laughed. "Robert, that is some of the finest information you could have given me. I had forgotten all about those operations, including the fact that the sale was still in negotiations."

"In all truthfulness, sir, you have been a bit preoccupied with the situation in New Hampshire," Robert reminded him.

"Yes, but it's no excuse not to do my job." Ezra sighed. "Still, that's fantastic news. Thank you. How are you and Abigail holding up?"

"Quite well, sir," Robert responded. "No news from any of the sentinels or from the searchers, either. I spoke briefly with Big Mike today."

"Hmm? How did that work out?"

"Fine," Robert chuckled. "It seems he still owed them for several jobs. Big-money jobs, as he described them. He wasn't too pleased about having to find new guys who would work as well as the Waverly brothers, but he did see the silver lining in the whole situation."

"That's good to hear. I am concerned, though, that no one else has seen Stan Owens," Ezra informed him. "We know he's in Norwich, I don't think it will take him much time to find us."

"We may be giving him too much credit, sir," Robert stated. "He is intelligent, and he is looking for us. But that doesn't mean he's going to narrow his search area to Norwich or even the outlying towns. He's going to understand that we are in a digital age and that we can reach out and try to touch him from just about anywhere there's a wireless signal."

"Very true, Robert."

"Other than this," Robert continued, "did any of the properties look promising?"

"Two did, which is better than I thought. This evening, I'll take a ride out to see what I can find out about how they look after dark," Ezra informed him.

"Very good, sir. Now, if you don't mind, I have a message to pass on from Abigail."

"Oh?" Ezra felt a smile tug at the corners of his mouth.

"Yes, she wants you to promise to be careful, sir. And she wants you to know she'll have a fresh coffee cake ready for when you return home."

Ezra laughed. "Thank her for me, please, Robert. I will call you both when I am preparing to fly home."

The men said their farewells, and Ezra was in a decidedly better mood when he set his phone down on the desk. He picked up the hotel room's phone, called down for room service, placed his order and then made his way to the shower. He would bathe, eat, and then nap. In the middle of the night, he would look at the two properties and hopefully make his decision in the morning about which would suit his needs better.

CHAPTER 25

A WALK WITH RAY

They were several miles from Tom's house, and Stan found himself enjoying the comfort of the dead man's presence. Ray, for his part, walked in silence, a soft smile on his face.

After almost an hour's worth of walking, Stan spoke. "Have you walked here on your own, within the range of your item?"

Ray nodded. "Plenty of times. I think it kept me from losing my mind. Strange to think about that, losing your mind after you're dead. But I walked. I found where animals bedded down and nested, and I figured out where to stand so I could watch them without scaring them off. Other days, I would sit in the weather and just watch it. I can't feel it, hot or cold or whatever it's doing at the time. It's strange, kind of like when I would watch television at my dad's house when I was a kid. Mom didn't like it much, so it was mostly at Dad's."

"Your parents were dead when you passed?" Stan asked.

"Yup. Mom had died in a car accident when I was twenty, and Dad had died of cancer the year after. Rough couple of years, but that was the way it went, you know?"

Stan nodded. He did know.

"I feel bad that people came and looked for me," Ray continued. "Kind of because they didn't find me. That would have been nice. Mostly because they put all that effort in and didn't find a damned thing. You know, the hunter who killed me, he was out here looking, too. Sort of like he was making sure nobody saw where he'd buried me."

Ray shrugged. "Anyway, after that, nobody worried about me. Lots of time to learn about this place. What about you? You got any relatives or anything?"

"No one who is alive," Stan answered. "At least, not anyone I know of. My parents died when I was young. The grandaunt and granduncle who took me in have both passed as well. I have several friends and a town but no direct family."

"A town?" Ray asked, grinning. "Did you just say you had a town?"

Stan nodded. "Yes. The town of Mason, New Hampshire. We look after one another. I help them when the dead become burdensome, and they help keep the world away from me."

"Is the world really that bad for you?"

"At times," Stan admitted.

"Yeah, I can see that," Ray nodded. "Life gets miserable. Even when you're dead."

"Yes," Stan agreed. "I have seen that, too."

They had tracked him for miles.

Literally for miles.

Stan Owens had traveled from Norwich to a small building some distance away. They were about to leave when Stan exited the building and started walking along the thin country road that passed by the structure.

And so they had followed him.

Oscar and Yancy had worked together for eight years, and that was after spending four years as cellmates. They know when to speak and when not to speak, when to act and when not to act. Theirs was a relationship born out of first necessity, then friendship, and finally comfort. Neither man had any real family left. Nor did either of them want to do much more than survive. The occasional odd job for Big Mike helped pay for the studio apartment they shared. The apartment itself was a comfort, seeing as how it was only slightly bigger than the cell they had shared. The kitchenette and the bathroom with the door on it were benefits, and the apartment had one wall tall enough to accommodate the surplus bunk bed.

Each man carried a .22 revolver. Nothing fancy. Nothing flashy. A .22 round to the head would kill a man just as easily as a .44. Their pistols were easy to hide on their bodies and easy to dispose of if necessary.

With any luck, they would kill Stan Owens and then dispose of the weapons far from where they'd drop the body if they had to take it from the crime scene.

It all depended on how much work they were going to have to put into it.

Once Stan Owens was a good distance away, the men exited Yancy's battered Camry. They closed the doors cautiously and then followed Owens. They could hear his voice as though he were carrying on a conversation.

"Do you think he's on a call?" Yancy asked.

"Maybe," Oscar answered. "We'll have to double-check before we do anything."

Yancy nodded.

They walked for an hour, always keeping a safe distance from the target.

"We should stop soon," Oscar stated. "We've gone pretty far from the car, and if some rural cop finds it, he's apt to try and figure out why it's parked on the side of the road."

Yancy grunted his agreement.

"Ten more minutes?" Oscar asked.

"Sure."

As soon as the words left his mouth, they caught sight of Stan Owens coming to a stop.

"Yes," Stan said, his voice no louder than a whisper. "We should return home."

Oscar and Yancy stepped off the road and into the woods. They eased down to the forest floor and prepared to ambush the target.

They would have to take pictures of the body for proof, but that was fine. Better than sawing off the head and bringing that back. That always left the men a little too tired.

Cutting through the bone was always difficult.

"You didn't see them."

Stan looked at Ray. "Who did I not see?"

"Two men behind us," the ghost answered. "Maybe a hundred feet or so. I'm impressed. They were damned quiet."

"Are they gone?" Stan asked.

Ray shook his head. "They're off on the right side of the road, in the woods. They only left the road when you said it was time to go back."

"I suspect they are looking for me, then," Stan stated.

Ray chuckled. "Probably. Want me to go have a look at them?"

"Yes, thank you."

"Tie your shoe or something," Ray advised.

"Why?" Stan asked, looking at his feet. "Both shoes are tied."

"To make it look like there's a reason why you stopped," the ghost chuckled.

"Ah. Yes, that would be sensible."

Stan squatted down and worked on shoelaces.

***

"How long does it take to tie a shoe?" Yancy muttered.

"Don't know," Oscar replied. "He's kind of obsessive with it."

Yancy grunted in agreement and then shivered. His body stiffened, and he glanced over at Oscar, who lay shaking as well.

"Cold front coming in?" Yancy asked.

"Hope not," Oscar answered. "It'll be a cold walk home."

Yancy looked back to the road and swore.

Stan Owens was gone.

Yancy reached over, slapped Oscar on the arm and pointed to where Owens had been.

Oscar shook his head and motioned for Yancy to stand up. In a moment, both men moved along the edge of the road, picking their way with care and keeping to the darkest shadows.

When they neared the place where Stan Owens had been, they found nothing. It was as though the man had simply disappeared.

Yancy put his pistol away, and Oscar did the same. There was only a slight chance someone other than Stan Owens was wandering around in the darkness, but neither Yancy nor Oscar was willing to risk killing the wrong person. The right person? Yes. But there was no guarantee now.

"Where could he have gone?" Oscar asked, his voice low.

Yancy began to answer him and something struck Oscar in the side of the head, knocking him down. Yancy reached into his pocket for the pistol as he crouched down, and a second object struck him in his left shoulder, numbing his arm and causing him to topple backward. Snarling, Yancy managed to draw the pistol, cocking the hammer back and looking around wildly for Stan Owens.

There was nothing to see. Nothing except darkness and his friend's body lying on the ground a few feet away. Yancy didn't know if Oscar was alive or dead, but he knew Stan Owens was to blame for his friend's condition.

Yancy twisted around, tried to get to his feet and felt a boot slam into his ribs. At least one of them cracked as the blow lifted him up, and then the boot came down on his hand, breaking his wrist and causing him to drop the pistol.

Yancy collapsed to the ground, unable to bear his own weight with the broken wrist and still numb arm. He rolled onto his side and looked up.

Stan Owens stood above him.

"I am not a good man," Stan stated, crouching down to pick up the .22 caliber pistol the stranger had dropped. "I know, too, that you are not a good man. You and your friend were sent to kill me. I am impressed. I did not notice you. It was Ray who did."

A gasp came from the first man Stan had struck, and a quick glance at the man, showed the damage the rock had caused.

"We're going to kill you," the other man hissed.

Stan shifted his attention back to that man.

"No, you are not," Stan told him. "I could, if you like, torture you for information. It would not be beneficial, however. I know you and your friend would invariably give me whatever information you thought I would believe in order for the pain to stop. I am, unfortunately, an old hand at this game. I know there is no information you can give me. There is nothing you know that will help me. You will not be allowed to live. I cannot risk having you making a second attempt on my life."

The reality of the situation settled around Yancy, and he looked to Oscar, not quite certain if it was really happening or not. The sight of Oscar taking short, rasping breaths solidified the reality of the situation.

Suddenly, Yancy wanted to live.

"I can tell you something, at least," Yancy offered, his voice taking on an unnatural whine.

"But there is nothing I want you to tell me," Stan told him. "Nothing I want to hear come out of your mouth."

"You can't kill us!" Yancy shouted. "Someone will find out, even if you hide the bodies!"

"I have no intention of hiding your bodies," Stan replied. "I do have every intention of making it look like a murder/suicide."

Yancy laughed, hysteria creeping into it. "How? What are you stupid? You can't use our guns against us!"

Stan crouched down and looked Yancy in the eye. "Do you really think this is the first murder/suicide I have planned out? Do you really believe there are mistakes I would make with something as simple as this?"

"I don't want to die," Yancy whispered.

"Few do," Stan replied. He lifted the .22, placed the muzzle against the man's temple and pulled the trigger.

CHAPTER 26
THE CEMETERY

They sat down on a picnic blanket spread beneath the wide boughs of a pine tree. Around them, across the landscaped and rolling grass, headstones cropped up and marched in long, neat rows. They were in a newer portion of the cemetery, one that did not have the twisting roads and leaning markers, the old slate with their dire warnings or the marbled effigies looking toward the heavens.

That would be for another day.

"This is beautiful," Lisbeth admitted. "I didn't think it would be this nice. There are a couple of great ones where I live, but nothing quite like this."

"I'm glad you like it," Tom grinned.

Lisbeth pulled her bag close to her, opened it, and began removing items. After several minutes, she had produced a thermos of coffee, cheese, crackers, and a variety of fruit.

"A real picnic," Tom laughed.

"When's the last time you were on a picnic like this?" Lisbeth asked, smiling.

Tom shook his head. "I don't know. Probably when I was a little boy, but I don't know."

"Fair enough." She took out a pair of cups from the bag, opened the thermos and poured out some coffee. "Do you mind if I ask you a personal question?"

"No, not at all."

"You talk about your dad but not your mom. Is she still around?"

Tom took a sip of coffee and then shook his head. "No. In fact, Victor is my adoptive father. When I was in high school, my biological mother and father were killed."

"I'm sorry," Lisbeth whispered.

"It's okay," Tom assured her. "It happened a long time ago, and they didn't like each other. I didn't want either of them dead, of course, but it wasn't like some great love affair was destroyed with their passing. Far from it. Anyway, lots of stuff happened, and I ended up living with Victor. He took care of me, brought me in and taught me everything he knows."

"Do you spend a lot of time with him?"

"Not as much as I would like." He took another drink. "He's suffering from severe Alzheimer's. He was assaulted by a person with a mental health issue, and he lost his eyes. My dad went downhill after that. So, he stays in a home in New London, and he doesn't remember me most days. In fact, he gets really upset when he sees me."

Lisbeth frowned, drank some of her own coffee and asked, "Why would that upset him?"

"Because he knows he should remember me. He knows I'm important to him, so his inability to remember makes him angry, and when he gets angry, he can lash out. Most of the time, it's against himself. I do go visit him, I just don't announce my presence. I sit and watch him talk with some of the other residents in his wing and with the staff. My dad's early Alzheimer's symptoms are rare, and I want to see if there's a way we can detect them even sooner. Maybe figure a way to slow down the process, give others a better quality of life."

"And that's why you go to school?" she asked.

Tom nodded and finished his coffee.

"That is absolutely amazing," she told him and leaned over the blanket to kiss him lightly on the cheek. "I don't think I've met anyone like you before, Tom. You're fantastic. Just absolutely fantastic."

Tom blushed. "Thanks. I don't think it's anything. It's what sons are supposed to do."

"What someone is supposed to do and what they do are usually two completely different things," she smiled.

Tom gave a quick nod and let the subject drop. He took a sip of coffee.

"Why did you pick a cemetery?" Lisbeth asked.

"The history," Tom answered. "Mostly for the history. There's the quiet, too. Plus, it reminds me of my friends and family who've passed, and I get to share some of my joy with them."

"Joy?" Lisbeth asked with a crooked smile.

"Happiness," Tom grinned. "Joy. Yeah. I don't get too much of that. At least, not lately. My dad's sick, I'm kind of arguing with another friend of mine."

Lisbeth raised an eyebrow, and Tom cleared his throat.

"So, um, there's this guy named Shane Ryan, and we've been friends for a long time. Something bad happened recently, and I got angry at him, even though it wasn't his fault."

"Have you apologized?" Lisbeth asked.

"I did, but the problem isn't Shane, it's me," Tom explained. "Everybody dies around Shane, and I don't want that anymore."

Her eyes widened slightly. "I'm sorry, Tom. I thought it was, I don't know, an argument over something silly."

He shook his head. "No. It's okay, I didn't explain what it was about, just that it was an argument. You don't have to apologize. It's hard, you know? I remember the people we knew, the people who were alive and then weren't."

"Is it okay if I ask you how they died?"

"They all died bad," Tom said, his voice husky. "Terrible. I saw it, and I'll never be able to unsee it. I don't know that I can deal with the violence anymore. It's why I don't talk to him that much."

"You still talk to this Shane Ryan?" she asked, surprised.

"Yeah. In fact, I'm helping another person because Shane asked me to." Tom looked down at the coffee cup in his hand and went silent.

"Hey," Lisbeth said, her voice soft. "How about we don't talk about it anymore right now? Let's talk about Steinbeck and what you want to do tonight."

"Tonight?" Tom asked, smiling.

"Tonight," Lisbeth nodded. "I want to spend a lot of time with you, Tom. I hope that's not weird."

"If it is, then we're both weird," he told her. "Because I want to spend a lot of time with you, too."

"Good." Lisbeth reached over and took his hand into hers. "Tell me what you like, Tom Daniels, and what you want out of life."

Tom swallowed nervously, smiled, and told her.

CHAPTER 27

SUCCESS

"It is, without any doubt, the best of all the options," Ezra stated.

"Excellent, sir," Robert nodded. "I did additional research and discovered the properties around the facility are available as well."

Ezra raised an eyebrow. "Is that so?"

"Yes. We can probably negotiate the prices down, too. It seems as though all the properties have been on the market for some time."

"One owner?"

"No," Robert answered with a shake of his head. "Three separate owners. Banks, actually, and the main property is owned by a credit union. Negotiations should be fairly straightforward. I suspect they've been paying a significant amount of taxes and insurance and will be pleased to let the properties go."

Ezra nodded his agreement. "Yes. Once we get the building and the properties around it, we'll need to get the proverbial boots on the ground for the preparation."

"And what preparation is that?" Abigail asked, carrying a tray of prepared sandwiches into the room.

"There is a new business venture I'm considering," Ezra stated. "And I'll need someone out there, at the new facility, to prepare for our transition."

"We're leaving this building?" she asked, unable to hide her surprise.

Ezra nodded. "This is a temporary fortification. I'd like to move the company to a more remote location. I won't ask you to come, Abigail, I know you've moved enough."

"Is that the facility you're talking about?" she asked, nodding toward the computer where a newer photo of the building was displayed.

"It is," Ezra confirmed. "The building needs some work, and there are other items that need to be taken care of. That's why I need someone there, on the ground, engaging with the workers and making sure all is kept on task."

"It's beautiful," Abigail murmured. "It reminds me of when my husband and I went on our honeymoon."

Neither Ezra nor Robert spoke.

She straightened up, turned to face them and declared, "I'll go."

Robert looked stunned, and Ezra asked, "Are you serious, Abigail?"

She nodded. "I think it would do me good to be there. Not only that, Mr. Pettigrew, but you need someone with exceptional logistic skills, and, quite frankly, that's me. I can have the building ready for your arrival, regardless of when that is. All I would need is to know what you want out of it."

Ezra chuckled and shook his head. "You are amazing, Abigail, and I know I don't tell you that often enough. I think it would be fantastic if you went ahead. You do have the best skills for this, and I would appreciate Robert being here. We have that last little detail to clean up regarding Stan Owens, and then we can move on to the next project."

Abigail beamed at them both. "Well, as soon as you have the details down, Mr. Pettigrew, I will book myself a flight, find a room to rent, and get down to brass tacks, as my mother used to say."

She nodded to them both, then turned around sharply on her heel and marched out of the room, closing the door behind her.

"I think she'll be brilliant, sir," Robert stated after a moment. "But she'll be frightening as well."

"Only to the employees," Ezra added. "And that will be the only thing we need to worry about. You know, I never even thought of asking Abigail to do it."

Robert chuckled. "Neither did I, sir."

Abigail returned a moment later with a small yellow legal pad and a pen. She took a seat, smiled and asked, "Will we be establishing an entirely new apparatus?"

"We will," Ezra confirmed.

She clicked the pen and wrote in her concise script across the top.

"We'll need bank accounts," Abigail stated and wrote it down. As she mentioned each necessity, she jotted it down as well. "Contractors from separate parts of the county, wherever it is. We'll get a couple of inspectors in as well. Suppliers for the basics, office equipment, too. I suspect we'll need living facilities if we're purchasing the property. If there's enough room, I'll look into having a house built. Do you want it multilevel, Mr. Pettigrew?"

He blinked, and Robert laughed.

Ezra grinned. "No, single level will be fine. I didn't see many two-story structures out there. I do want a good-sized pantry."

"I am assuming you mean a separate building for emergency supplies?"

Ezra chuckled and nodded.

Abigail wrote down several more items, and when she looked up, she had a broad smile on her face. She clicked the pen once more, put it away and looked from Robert to Pettigrew. "When I was a younger woman, I would imagine what it would be like to plan out an entire town. Sort of an end-of-the-world preppers town."

"I don't know that we'll go that far, Abigail," Ezra stated. "But I think you should definitely lay in supplies for at least a month for the three of us."

"We'll have supplies for longer than that, Mr. Pettigrew," she said, getting to her feet. "And I'll get them at a cost that'll be less than a month's."

She nodded to them both and exited the room once more.

Her confidence left the men in shock, and a moment later, Ezra felt a rising sense of home.

With Robert and Abigail beside him, anything would be possible.

✳ ✳ ✳

Mr. Pettigrew had gone home hours earlier, and Robert sat alone in the office. When his phone rang, he fully expected it to be his employer with one last request for the day.

It was not Mr. Pettigrew.

It was Big Mike's personal phone.

"Yes?" Robert answered.

"I'm missing two more guys," Big Mike responded, his voice low and heavy. "Had 'em slap one of those Apple air tags up under the dashboard. They've been parked in one spot for too long. Last I heard from them, they'd figured out where your big ticket guy is at. I ain't sending anybody out there. Ain't got anybody to send. Guys are running from this job now, and I don't blame 'em."

"Send me the location, Big Mike," Robert told him, keeping his tone conciliatory. "I'll go check it out in the morning and let you know what I find out."

"Sure." Big Mike read out the numbers, and Robert jotted them down. "Listen, I'll give you a call if they get in touch or if the car starts to move. Pretty sure you're going to find both of 'em dead, though. Just like everybody else. Who is this guy anyway? Some secret agent, special forces guy?"

"No," Robert sighed. "He's just someone from New Hampshire."

"Screw that state, then," Big Mike snorted. "I ain't leavin' Connecticut."

They ended the call, and Robert decided he would sleep in the office for the night. It would be easier to leave from there than his apartment.

He sent a quick text to Mr. Pettigrew and then went about getting ready for bed.

CHAPTER 28
YANCY

Yancy woke up with a headache. One that rivaled the worst he'd ever had before, and that had been from a long night of drinking rotgut whiskey in the back of Mary Sullivan's Fiero. None of that had worked out the way he had planned.

With a groan, he rolled onto his side and reached for his phone, slapping at the floor where he usually kept it.

When he couldn't find it, he opened his eyes and looked around, confused.

He wasn't home.

He was in some woods, and he couldn't see anything other than trees and the ground. There wasn't even anything to hear. No birds, no squirrels. Not a damned thing.

Grumbling to himself, he sat up, trying to remember what it was he had done the night before. Where had he gone with Oscar?

His eyes came to rest on a pair of bodies, and it took him only a moment to recognize one as Oscar's. Oscar was slumped on one side, a .22 near his hand, a large rock a short distance away. A second body was a few feet away. There was a bullet hole in the temple, and as Yancy took a cautious step forward, he identified it.

He was looking at his own corpse.

Yancy stared, his mind failing to comprehend what he was looking at. After a moment, he shook his head and turned his back on the corpses.

As fear surged through him, he patted his body, but he could hardly feel it. He knew it was there, but it didn't seem right. Nothing felt right.

He staggered around, searching for the road. His mind, numb and confused, raced back and forth over the memories of the day before. He needed to know what he had been doing. Where he and Oscar had gone.

For several long minutes, Yancy clambered through the woods, and soon, he could see a break in the tree line. Ahead of him was a field, and beyond that, the road.

Sobbing with relief, he hurried forward and then stopped. His legs would not move him forward. He stepped to the right, and then to the left, and then back. All of this was fine.

He simply could not go forward.

Yancy put his hands against his head and then felt something that shouldn't have been there.

A hole in his temple.

Small and neat, he probed it with his finger, pushing it in until it could no longer move forward. After a moment, he withdrew the digit and looked at it. There was nothing on it, although it should have been covered in blood.

He lowered his hand and remembered the fight.

The target, Stan Owens, had ambushed them. He had gotten the drop on them, and that had been that.

"I was killed with Oscar's gun," Yancy whispered. "Stan Owens did it. He made it look like a murder suicide."

Just like he said he would.

Yancy looked around, tried to step forward again, but he was stopped by an invisible wall.

Somehow, he couldn't leave. He was tethered to his body. Was this Hell? Would he be by himself forever? Was Oscar in another Hell?

Did Hell really exist?

Confused, Yancy turned and walked to the right, keeping his shoulder against the unseen wall. He didn't count his footsteps or anything else that might help him measure the distance because that didn't matter.

He needed to know how far he could go, and within a few minutes, he discovered he couldn't go very far at all.

Yancy reached a corner, turned and followed it. He did it twice more and found himself back in the same field, able to look out but not cross that unseen line.

"Where am I?" he whispered. "What's going on?"

He held back a scream, turned and ran back to where he had awakened.

The bodies were still there, and the scream Yancy had been trying to contain finally broke loose.

Stan had found the men's car and left it where it was. He had no need to move it. No desire to see what might be inside of it. From the bodies of the men, he had collected a pair of phones identical to the others, and he had left them for Tom to look at. When Stan finished his breakfast and his morning tea, he left a note stating that he was going for a walk and then did exactly that.

He was a few minutes down the road when Ray appeared.

"It's nice to see new surroundings," Ray stated.

"I can imagine it was difficult remaining in one place for a significant period of time," Stan told him.

"It was," Ray nodded. "But you get used to it. I mean, you get used to anything, really. And there were some days where I slept. Probably slept entire weeks and months. It's hard to judge time. About the only way I could do so was through the change of the seasons, and even then, if I slept a year or two, things would really be out of whack."

Stan did not answer, for there was no question asked.

"So, where are we headed today?"

"Along the same road," Stan informed him. "I am curious as to how long it will take for the bodies to be found."

"How come?"

"You were there for a long time," Stan replied.

"Yeah, but I was buried. You left them out in the open."

"True," Stan nodded. "It is my hope they will be discovered sooner rather than later."

"You're not worried about being a suspect?"

Stan shook his head. "I have already established a routine. I walk this way each morning and in the evening. Sometimes more than that. People who drive this route regularly, including police officers, have observed this."

"Won't you be suspect if you don't report the car?"

Again, Stan shook his head. "No. I am a New Englander. I am an older New Englander. It would be more suspect if I were to put my nose into business that was not mine."

Ray chuckled. "Yeah, you're not wrong about that. And you're not going to discover the bodies?"

"No," Stan told him. "I have no desire to go anywhere near the bodies. I only want to walk my route. To stop doing so would bring attention to me, which is what I wish to avoid."

A howl tore through the air, and they stopped to listen.

"That is a cry from the dead," Stan observed.

"Yeah," Ray frowned. "Except there shouldn't be anyone out here."

Stan sighed. "Perhaps they're new."

"How could there…" Ray stopped and nodded. "Right. The two guys from yesterday."

"Yes. The two from yesterday."

"I'll check it out," Ray stated.

Stan nodded and stepped off the road. He started walking straight into the woods as the dead man raced off. Ray would cover the distance between the road and the bodies quickly, and Stan wondered if both men or only one had awakened from death to discover he was less than he was before.

He walked for another five minutes before he caught a glimpse of Ray. One of the men Stan had killed walked beside Ray, a look of bewilderment on the newly dead man's face.

When they came to a stop a few feet from Stan, the dead man blinked, focused on Stan and whispered, "You."

"Me," Stan nodded. "You have not moved on."

The dead man shook his head.

"What is your name?"

The stranger licked his lips, hesitated and then said, "Yancy."

Stan nodded. "A pleasure to meet you, Yancy."

The dead man laughed. "A pleasure? How can this be a pleasure?"

"It is a pleasure because I am not dead."

Yancy blinked as anger clouded his features. Then, the emotion drained out of his face. "Yeah. Guess you're right about that."

"Would you like to talk?" Stan asked, sitting down.

The dead men did the same.

"Why?" Yancy asked.

"Why did you not move on?"

Yancy nodded.

"I do not have an answer for you, I am afraid," Stan admitted. "I can assure you I have searched for that answer, yet in no place does it seem to be found. Some move on to whatever awaits them. Others do not. There seems to be no rhyme, no reason to it."

"Me and Oscar, we were supposed to kill you."

"I know," Stan replied.

"And you're not mad about it?" Yancy asked.

"Why would I be mad?" Stan asked. "You were not successful in your attempt. Nor were the others who came before you. I am hopeful that those who come after will not succeed, either."

"Are you good at killing?" Yancy asked, and both he and Ray looked at Stan.

"Yes," Stan nodded. "I am. What is worse, gentlemen, is that I enjoy it."

CHAPTER 29
UNBELIEVABLE

While Robert was not overly fond of urban life, he was in love with nature.

He had grown up hunting, fishing and camping. His years with his family in the wilderness on the weekends and over vacations had instilled a deep love for the outdoors in him, one he nurtured whenever he could.

Word had come earlier in the morning that two more of Big Mike's hired help had gone missing, but there was information as to where they were supposed to be. And so, Robert had driven the two hours to get there, and he had found the men's car. He had been looking for it on foot when he caught sight of Stan Owens.

Robert had been ready to duck into the woods on the opposite side of the road when Owens had turned sharply and marched off into the tree line. The mechanical nature of the movement reminded Robert of a windup toy, and before he could stop himself, he was following Owens.

Robert kept a fair distance from him, moving easily from tree to tree, always with an eye on where Owens was going. The man walked for nearly ten minutes, and Robert was about to turn back when Owens stopped, and the air shimmered around him.

A heartbeat later, a pair of men appeared. Both were undeniably dead.

One man with a long beard had a hole in his chest. The other, dressed for a walk through the city, had a small hole in his temple. The bearded man looked comfortable, pleasant as he sat down across from Stan Owens. He guided the other ghost into a sitting position.

That ghost, the one with the hole in his head, did not look comfortable. He looked confused.

Robert crept closer, a few inches at a time, straining to hear what was being said.

"...I enjoy it."

Owens' words drifted out to him.

"You enjoy it?" the man with the hole in his head asked.

"I enjoy it, Yancy," Owens nodded. "This is an issue that I must deal with, and it has taken me a long time to even come to grips with saying that fact, let alone allowing myself to think it."

"I didn't like it," Yancy said, his voice waxing and waning. "It was just part of the job. And not even all the time."

"I like it. I learned to like it," Owens continued. "It was the only way I could deal with what I had to do as a teen. Still, there must have been something in me that enjoyed the act to begin with."

Robert brought his phone out, saw the ghosts were too far from him to drain the phone's battery, and started to record the meeting.

"How many?" Yancy asked.

"How many what?" Stan replied.

"Killed!" Yancy snapped, snarling. "How many have you killed, you psycho!"

"I do not know," Stan answered. "I stopped counting at one hundred."

"And when was that, huh?"

"I was sixteen," Stan told him. "I did not wish to remember their faces anymore."

"What?" Yancy's voice was difficult to hear.

"I killed to survive," Stan continued. "I would have been killed in turn if I had failed, and so I did not fail. When I became weak, when I feared for my soul, I locked it away so it could be blackened any further. I forced myself to enjoy what I did. Not to revel in it. To take satisfaction in a job well done. To know I alone could do the things I was tasked with."

"You're a monster," Yancy said, his voice flat.

"Yes," Stan nodded. "I have never claimed to be otherwise."

"No wonder they want you dead."

"I think they want him dead because of what he can do," the bearded ghost interjected. "Not because of what he did. I'm pretty sure the guys who hired you weren't doing it to get rid of a problem for society."

"It doesn't matter," Yancy said, jabbing a finger at the bearded one. "Owens deserves to die."

"All of us do," Stan stated. "When it is my time to die, I will. Until then, I will continue on with my purpose."

"I don't know what you think your purpose is," Yancy snarled, getting to his feet. "But I know what mine is now."

"And what is that?" Stan asked, remaining seated.

"To kill you!" Yancy howled and launched himself at Owens.

Owens didn't move, and when the ghost struck him, Yancy disappeared.

The bearded one looked at Owens in surprise and asked the question Robert wanted to ask.

"What happened?"

"He touched me," Stan answered, getting to his feet. "It is not a wise decision for the dead to do so."

"Why's that?" the ghost asked.

"I am riddled with iron," Stan replied. "There is no safe way for a ghost to touch me. The iron in my flesh will cast them back to their object. And since this is what has happened to Yancy, it would be a good time to return to the road. Was he close enough to it to be a problem?"

The bearded ghost shook his head. "Nope. Not even when he gets his full strength."

"Good," Stan nodded. "It is unfortunate he will be alone, but perhaps that is what he needs."

Robert turned off the phone and slipped around the opposite side of the tree as Stan Owens and the ghost returned to the road. Robert would do the same in a short time, but he needed to give them space, and to process what he had witnessed and heard.

If the dead truly couldn't touch Owens, how was anything being planned going to stop him?

CHAPTER 30

A FEMALE VISITOR

"This is amazing," Lisbeth said, looking around the room as Tom closed the door behind her.

"Do you think so?" he asked and winced at his own worried tone.

She turned, smiled and nodded. "I wouldn't say it if I didn't mean it. I've been told that I'm brutally honest at times."

"Oh yeah?"

"Yeah," she laughed. "I tell them it's not honesty, it's just an inability to keep my mouth shut."

Tom chuckled and led her through the different display cases. About halfway through the room, she stopped and looked down into a case.

"What is that?" she asked, pointing at a small dark shape hidden by hair.

Tom glanced over her shoulder and answered. "That's a shrunken head."

"Really?!" Lisbeth leaned closer, resting her hands on the wood casing. "Can I ask why its face is hidden? Is it a little creepy?"

Tom hesitated, then replied, "This might sound strange, but he doesn't like to be face up."

Lisbeth turned and grinned at him. "Are you telling the truth?"

Tom nodded, his face flushed. "Yeah. He's Maori, and he speaks a bit of English, but not too much. Enough to be able to tell me he doesn't like to be face up."

"Why?"

"Well, a Maori's tattoos represent that person's history. He was a warrior, and when he died in battle, the man who killed him did what all the Maori did. He collected his head. This man's head showed others that the man who killed him had defeated a powerful enemy. And that was fine. He didn't have a problem with having his head collected; after all, that was the way things were done."

Tom tapped the glass. "This guy, he had evidently killed a lot of people, and the daughter of one of the men he had killed was upset. So, when no one was looking, she went and cut the tattoo celebrating her father's death off this guy's face."

"This man," Lisbeth said, gesturing toward the head. "What's his name?"

"He won't tell me," Tom answered. "He said he won't say his name because it was stolen when the tattoo was removed from him."

"Oh."

Tom nodded. "Yeah. He sulks a lot. I wish he didn't, I'd love to learn more about him. But I don't want to pester him, either. They need their time, too."

Lisbeth stepped closer, gently pulled his head down and kissed Tom.

"You are fantastic, Tom Daniels," she told him, looking into his eyes. "I don't know anyone, anyone at all, who would do that for a ghost."

He kissed her and smiled. "Thank you. Come on, I'll show you the rest of the house."

She slipped her arm around his waist, and they went toward the kitchen together.

They lay on the couch, his prosthetic on the coffee table and empty teacups beside it.

"Your heart's strong," she murmured.

"Is it?" he asked, his eyes closed.

"It sounds like thunder," Lisbeth told him, pressing her ear closer to his chest. "I love it."

"I'm glad. I love the way you smell."

She giggled. "I have never heard anyone say that before."

"No?"

"Nope. I've been told I stink like a hippie," she sighed.

"I've smelled hippies," Tom stated. "You definitely do not smell like one."

"What does a hippie even smell like?"

"The hippie kids at my high school smelled like patchouli and body odor," he chuckled. "They didn't believe in deodorant. Said it wasn't natural."

She gave an exaggerated shudder. "They didn't believe in natural deodorants?"

"Nope. So, between the patchouli, the body odor and whatever quality marijuana they were smoking, there was generally a tough smell that followed them around." He kissed the top of her head, grinned and added, "You could see the cloud."

"Shut up."

"No, for real," he lied. "It was like mustard gas in World War One. This pea green soup colored cloud that just rolled along behind them."

"You're the best, Tom," she whispered, pulling the blanket that covered them up higher around her shoulders. "I'm kind of upset, though."

"Why?" He opened his eyes and looked down at her as she, in turn, looked up at him.

"It's taken us years to find each other," she said, her tone serious. "Years lost."

He shook his head. "They weren't lost. They helped make us who we are. If we didn't have those years behind us, we might not be here right now. And I can't think of anything worse than that."

"You're right," she nodded after a moment. "There isn't anything worse than that."

She closed her eyes and nestled against him. Tom smiled, closed his eyes and traced the small of her back with his fingers.

The call of a raven pierced the stillness and lulled them both to sleep.

CHAPTER 31
DISCUSSIONS AMONGST SISTERS

"Where have you been?" Morrigan asked.

On the other end of the video call, Lisbeth towel dried her hair and grinned at her sister. "In the last half hour or so? The shower."

"It's almost midnight, you brat," Morrigan laughed. "You were supposed to call earlier."

"Yeah, I know." Lisbeth wrapped the towel around her head, tucked the end in and dropped down into a chair in the hotel room. She leaned forward, adjusted the camera and stifled a yawn. "I was at Tom's."

"Tom, the one you have an interest in?"

Lisbeth's face reddened. "I think it's a little more than an interest. He's just brilliant, Sis. Absolutely brilliant."

Morrigan raised an eyebrow and took three sips of tea from her cup. "How long were you there?"

"Most of the day," she admitted. "I'm going back tomorrow."

"Did you get a look at the collection?"

Lisbeth nodded. "It's huge. Three, maybe four times the Kelliher collection."

Morrigan lowered the teacup. "Really? That large?"

"Yup. He told me that's not all of it, either. There's another set sealed in the basement of the church. Ones that really don't want to be bothered. The ones in display cases still like to get a bit of sunlight and get let out once in a blue moon."

"Church?" Morrigan asked. "What church?"

"That's where he lives," Lisbeth answered. "An old converted church.

There's the main display area, where the pews were, the kitchen, which is where the pulpit was, and then a bathroom and a couple of bedrooms and a den."

"You really saw the whole place," Morrigan smirked.

Lisbeth's face reddened again. "Yeah. Spent most of the time in the den."

"Watching television or playing board games?" Morrigan asked with mock innocence.

Lisbeth laughed and shook her head. "Yeah, I'm not going to answer that."

"You don't have to," Morrigan smiled. "Anyway, if he has overflow, do you think he would be open to passing along some of his stock?"

"I don't know," Lisbeth replied. "I mean, he doesn't look at them like stock. He sees them as people still. He knows almost all of them by name, and he knows their histories. It's really impressive."

"I'm sure it is."

"You're not thinking of having me ask about the items, are you?"

The note of worry in Lisbeth's voice caused Morrigan to pause and then shake her head.

"No, of course not," Morrigan answered. "I told you before that we don't need to bring it up. It's just the businesswoman in me looking for new suppliers. That's all."

"What about the whole Ezra Pettigrew situation?" Lisbeth asked, deftly changing the subject.

Morrigan grinned at her sister. "Oh, I'm just waiting for him to pressure the dead. He's not going to like the fact that they won't listen to him."

"Do you think he'll be able to pressure them?"

Morrigan shook her head. "I think he'll try to harm them. That's for certain. However, the ones I sent him, even if he does threaten, they'll be happy to go. They're the ones who are too tired to ask for destruction."

Lisbeth nodded, rubbed her eyes and yawned.

"You need to go to sleep," Morrigan told her. "It seems like you did a lot today."

Lisbeth blushed again. "You're a brat."

"Yup."

"Okay. I'll give you a call tomorrow," Lisbeth said, bringing the phone closer.

"Don't set a time," Morrigan replied. "Call when you can. I don't want you worrying about talking to me if you're having a good time with Tom, okay?"

"Okay, sis," Lisbeth answered and yawned once more. "Talk soon."

"Good night."

Morrigan ended the call and took three more sips of her cold tea.

She didn't want Lisbeth to pressure Tom Daniels, but having him as a resource would work well. However, she would need to convince him that the ghosts he let go would be better off. He seemed like the type, but she wouldn't be sure until she could meet him in person.

And that might take a bit of time since she had to worry about Pettigrew.

Then again, Lisbeth really liked him, and Morrigan might meet him sooner than she thought.

Humming, she stood and cleaned her dishes. Despite the late hour, there were still chores to finish.

Chapter 32
Telephone

"Stan!"

Stan looked up from his book, put the bookmark into place and set it down before replying, "Yes?"

"Come in here," Tom called from his room. "I found something!"

The excitement in the young man's voice put some speed into Stan's movements as he got up and left his own room, buttoning his suitcoat as he went.

"What is it?" he asked, stopping just behind and to the right of Tom.

"Here," Tom answered, highlighting a section of the text on the screen. "This tells me, right here, that all the phones, every single one of them, were sent to the same store."

Stan glanced at the pile of phones on the table beside the desk. "Each of them?"

Tom nodded. "Yes. I have the basic information. What company they came from, and the fact that they were shipped out as one unit. The only thing I don't know yet is where they were sold from. But all these numbers, see how they're in sequential order?"

"Yes."

"And this number here, I found out, means that this is one lot being sold to one specific location. That location has to be around here because all the other information we have on these guys is that they're local."

"Local as to the city of Norwich?" Stan asked.

"I don't know," Tom answered. "If not Norwich, then definitely one of the cities around us. Maybe New London or Willimantic. I don't think they're coming from as far as New Haven or Hartford, but those might be possibilities."

"Is there a chance the phones might have been sourced from a much farther location?" Stan asked.

Tom grinned. "There's always a chance, but I don't think it's likely. Most people aren't going to think about where they're buying one lot of phones from. Plus, I don't think Pettigrew expected you to be able to track them down through the phones."

"He is correct," Stan stated. "I am not able to do so. It is why I came to see you, Tom. I am inept regarding the use of computers."

Tom chuckled. "Anyway, I'll keep working on this. What are you going to do?"

"I am going to make a pot of tea," Stan told him. "Would you care for some?"

"No," Tom replied. "I'm all set with that. I'm going to focus on the phones."

Stan nodded and left the room for the kitchen. In a few minutes, he had the kettle going, and he stood by the counter. Later in the evening, he would, he hoped, speak with Gwen. A small smile crept onto his face as he thought of her and realized how much he missed her.

He missed Mason, New Hampshire, as well. The comforts of his room, the familiarity of the streets, the ritualistic acts of eating his meals at the diner. Even seeing the ghost of his grandaunt. These were all facets of his life he was missing.

And then, too, there was Adam.

The young man remained in the ICU, and if the dead had spoken the truth, he would soon be among them.

Stan wasn't sure how he felt about the situation.

In one sense, it would be best for Adam to die if there was no hope for his recovery. On the other, Stan did not want to lose a friend.

A well of sadness, long since covered after the death of his parents, threatened to rise up and wash over him. Stan knew he would need to keep the pressure upon that metaphoric well. If he did not, the decades of sadness and horror might drown him in grief.

As these thoughts overtook him, the image of Gwen smiling at him came into view, and he closed his eyes to enjoy it. A sense of calm moved up from the depths and comforted him. He could smell her hair, feel her skin, and hear her voice in his memory.

The kettle whistled, and Stan opened his eyes.

He would need to end Pettigrew quickly. He missed Gwen, and he wanted to be home.

Stan turned off the heat beneath the kettle and poured the water into the pot. As the tea steeped, he considered how best to destroy Pettigrew.

CHAPTER 33
A FAVORABLE REPORT

Abigail stood in the main office of the building Mr. Pettigrew had purchased for his future business endeavor.

He had been right, of course. The building was perfect. Structurally, it was sound, there had been no damage from the elements. The company that had owned it had indeed kept it in good condition. And, as Robert had surmised, the holder of the deed had been all too happy to rid themselves of the tax burden. The nearby properties had sold out as well, and Mr. Pettigrew had saved a healthy amount of money. Especially since he had paid cash.

Abigail looked over the main office, jotting down notes on her pad as she went. The carpeting would need to be removed and replaced with tile. Hideous fluorescents would need to be replaced with cheaper and far more enjoyable LEDs. The walls had to be checked for insulation, and all the outlets and basic electronics, of course.

But Abigail had been pleased to see there was no sign of animal or insect infestation. Whoever had worked as the caretaker had done well, and Abigail wrote a note to herself as a reminder to see who it was. If he or she couldn't be convinced to work for Mr. Pettigrew in the same capacity, then that person at least should receive a healthy bonus.

Abigail glanced at her watch. Almost noon, which meant it was almost time to call Mr. Pettigrew and Robert with an update.

She smiled at the thought of Robert. They had both lost their spouses long ago, and a fine friendship had formed between them. It would never move beyond that, and the two of them were happy with the arrangement.

Neither could stand the thought of remarrying, and their friendship deterred other widows and widowers from making an effort to engage in a relationship. They all believed that Abigail and Robert were an "item", as the saying went.

Shaking her head at the silliness of it all, Abigail left the office and walked toward her rental car. It was time to make the call.

The call came in exactly when Abigail said it would, and Ezra smiled. She was punctual as well as skilled, and you could, if you desired, set your watch by her routines.

Ezra did not. Her adherence was comforting but nothing for him to focus too much on.

So long as it continued, and he highly doubted anything could interrupt her. Abigail was a force of nature.

Robert leaned forward and answered the call. Ezra listened as they engaged in the pleasantries, and a moment later, she addressed herself to him.

"Mr. Pettigrew," she smiled, "the situation is even better than I could have hoped for."

"Is that so?"

She nodded. "I was afraid that after several years of sitting empty, we would have been looking at all kinds of damages. The sorts of damages that would make a deal like this worthless, regardless of how much they tried to get rid of it for."

"Tell me what you found." He and Robert listened as she filled them in on the status of the building. When she finished, he looked at Robert and saw the man was beaming.

"This is great news, sir," Robert nodded. "I can't even tell you how good this is."

"I will take your word for it," Ezra replied, glancing from Robert to the screen. "Both of yours. I am extremely pleased this is working out so far. Have you made any connections with the local banking communities?"

Abigail shook her head. "That is for tomorrow. Once I finish with the bankers, I will move on to the contractors we'll need to sort out any minor repairs."

"Brilliant, Abigail," Ezra said, congratulating her. "This is great work, and I truly appreciate it."

"I'm happy to do it, sir," she replied. "I really enjoy being out here, and I have the feeling I'll enjoy overseeing the project, too."

"I'm sure you will," Ezra agreed. "Now, is there anything you need? Anything we forgot in the initial planning."

She raised an eyebrow. "Mr. Pettigrew, I don't forget details. Not with my planning."

Ezra held up his hands, sufficiently chastised. "Mea culpa, Abigail. Mea culpa."

"Is there anything else we're forgetting, Abigail?" Robert asked.

"No, I think we're all right at the moment," she answered. "All I need at this point is the go-ahead to start negotiations and awarding contracts."

"By all means," Ezra replied. "You have carte blanche, Abigail, and my complete trust."

She flashed a proud, satisfied smile at them both, bade them a good night and signed off.

When Robert had turned the phone off, he chuckled when he looked at Ezra. "That place will be perfect by the time we get there, sir."

"I have no doubt about it," Ezra agreed. "Now, to shift the subject slightly. Has there been any word about the missing men?"

Robert frowned and nodded. "They were found about half an hour ago. Our operative states it's being looked at as a murder-suicide."

"Could it have been?" Ezra asked.

"Of course, it could have been," Robert answered. "I don't think so, though. Not with finding Stan Owens close by. I think he managed to kill them and stage it."

"As do I," Ezra sighed. "If there's any change, let me know. Regardless of the time."

"Of course, sir."

Ezra stretched. "I'm returning to my apartment. I'll have the phone on should you need anything."

"All right, sir."

Ezra smiled, stood up and left the office. As he walked down the stairs, he thought about the situation with Owens and wondered if it might not be time to leave and start over completely.

CHAPTER 34

A MEETING OF THE MINDS

It was not an establishment Ezra would normally have visited. The building stank, the lights were too dim, and there was nothing on the menu that looked even remotely palatable. Even the listed drinks sounded atrocious.

He walked to the bar, unbuttoned his coat and took a seat on one of the cleaner barstools.

A man with a pronounced limp and a wide nose came over to him, his nostrils flaring as if smelling the difference between the two of them.

"What are you drinking?" the bartender asked.

"Whiskey, neat," Ezra answered. "And I'm here to speak with Big Mike."

"Are you now?" The bartender glanced over his shoulder. "He's busy for another ten minutes at least. You may want more than one drink. He tends to be a little rough 'round this time in the evening."

Ezra resisted any sort of sarcastic answer and nodded. The attitude he had with his peers might not work well in the present company.

The bartender stepped away and returned a moment later with his drink. Ezra took out his money clip and pulled out a twenty, laying it down on the bar top.

"I'll get your change," the bartender told him and picked up the bill.

Ezra shook his head. "No. Keep it."

The man raised an eyebrow. "That's a helluva tip, mister."

"You pay for good service," Ezra replied.

The bartender chuckled, folded the money into the palm of his hand

and walked away.

Ezra neither nursed the drink nor did he knock it back. He drank it at a steady pace, and when he finished, he ordered another.

Ezra was close to finishing the second when the bartender walked over to him.

"Big Mike's ready," the man said and nodded toward a small door set to the left of a pinball machine.

"Thanks," Ezra replied and climbed off the stool.

"Sure. Name's Ralph, by the way," the bartender stated and offered his hand.

Ezra shook it, nodding. "Ezra."

"Pleasure. Remember, he's a bit of a bear. Go slow."

"Thank you."

Ezra walked across the room, knocked on the door and waited. A moment later, a heavy voice answered, "Come in."

Ezra did as commanded, finding it strange to be at someone else's beck and call. He knew it was only for a short time, but it reminded him of his youth, just starting out in the world of business.

And he didn't like it.

Ezra closed the door behind him and looked at the man sitting in a large chair behind an equally large desk. A bright fluorescent light suspended from the ceiling cast its harsh glow over the room, giving Big Mike a sickly appearance, one highlighted by the sheen of sweat on his bald head.

"Sit down, Mr. Pettigrew."

Ezra did so, ignoring the discomfort of the old office chair.

"What brings you here?" Big Mike asked, picking up a pack of cigarettes and shaking one out. "I got to be honest, I didn't ever expect to see you. Maybe Robert, I talk to him enough, but not you."

"I thought it would be a good time to meet," Ezra explained.

Big Mike, whose massive frame filled his own chair, grinned, flashing several gold teeth. "I appreciate that. You need another drink or anything?"

Ezra shook his head. "No, thank you."

"Damn, hotter in hell tonight," Big Mike muttered, unbuttoning the top button on his dark blue dress shirt. "HVAC system's been on the fritz lately. One of those things that got to wait, though, you know?"

"I do, but you don't have to wait." Ezra didn't know if he wanted to impress Big Mike or if he was feeling magnanimous from the whiskey, but he took out his phone and sent a quick text to Robert. The reply returned less than a minute later as Big Mike watched in silence.

"Excellent," Ezra said, returning his phone to his pocket. "My HVAC company will be here in the next half hour. They'll get it sorted for you."

"What's it going to cost me?" Big Mike asked, his tone cautious.

"Nothing," Ezra answered, and he held up a forestalling hand. "And not a favor in the future, either. We've had a good relationship thus far, Big Mike, and I would like that to continue. I own the business, it won't cost me more than a few extra hours of overtime and a bit of material at cost. What it will do is help you, just as you've helped me. I'm sorry we lost the Waverly brothers."

Big Mike grunted his agreement. "Those boys were good at what they did, but there are always others. Anything else you need, Ezra?"

"No. Do you have anything you need?"

Big Mike hesitated, then nodded. "Hell, it can't hurt to ask. I heard you've got a guy on the inside of the Norwich Police Department. That truc?"

"We have people on most of the police departments in the places we operate in," Ezra confirmed. "It's good business practice."

"Yup. Well, I got a problem in Norwich. There's a leak on my narcotics side, and I don't know who's feeding the cops their intel. It's damned good." The chair creaked as Big Mike shifted his weight. "What I need is to know who it is. Once I do, I can plug the leak."

"Are you going to kill the person?" Ezra asked.

"Would it bother you?"

Ezra shook his head. "No. I just want to know what to expect. Deaths bring their own risks."

Big Mike chuckled. "You're right about that. No, it doesn't work as well as isolating the leak. We feed them bad intel for a bit, the cops lose faith, the leak gets upset, and they eventually leave. If they're a constant problem, one of the regular plants the state uses, then we'll put the word out. Someone else will take care of them. That leaves my hands clean. I got enough going on without worrying about an accessory to murder charge."

"Agreed. Well, let me see what I can do," Ezra told him. "I'll have Robert ask, and when he has an answer, he'll reach out to you. Fair enough?"

"Hell, yes, it is," Big Mike laughed. He stood up, and for the first time, Ezra got a glimpse of how truly big the man was.

Big Mike stood close to seven feet tall, and Ezra suspected he was well over three hundred pounds, very little of which was fat. The man offered his hand, and Ezra's own disappeared into it when they shook.

"You know," Big Mike said, letting go of his hand, "you got a good name out there."

"Really?" Ezra asked.

Big Mike nodded. "Oh yeah. You pay your bills on time, you do what you say, and you never rat on anybody. Pretty damned solid. And this business with the HVAC, that's about as standup as they come, Ezra. I appreciate it."

Big Mike walked him to the door, opened it, and everyone in the bar looked over.

"Ralph," Big Mike called, and the bartender straightened up.

"Yeah, boss?"

"Mr. Pettigrew here drinks for free. Forever," Big Mike stated.

Ralph gave a thumbs up, and Big Mike clapped Ezra on the back with enough force to shake him where he stood.

"Drink up, Ezra, whenever you want."

"I will," Ezra assured him. "For now, I think I'll have one or two more. I want to make sure the boys get here soon."

"I'm sure they will," Big Mike chuckled and withdrew into his office.

Ezra returned to the bar and Ralph brought him a whiskey, neat. When Ezra placed a twenty on the bar, Ralph shook his head. "You drink for free, Ezra. You heard Big Mike."

"Yes, I heard him," Ezra nodded. "I drink for free. It doesn't mean I don't tip."

Ralph grinned as he picked up the money from the bar. "I understand, Mr. Pettigrew. You let me know if you need another one. Or anything else, for that matter."

Ezra smiled, nodded and took a drink. For a brief moment, he considered how difficult it might be to kill Morrigan and seize her stock. Would it be worth the effort? Would he even be able to utilize all her stock?

He would think about it as he waited for the HVAC crew, and he would drink as he did so.

CHAPTER 35

TELEPHONES

Tom straightened up, shook his head and muttered, "No way."

He clicked magnify on the screen, and the enlarged font only confirmed what he had read a heartbeat before.

A laugh escaped his lips, and he stood up, the tension and tiredness vanishing.

"Stan!" he yelled. "I found them!"

Stan's methodical steps rang out on the wooden floor, and then he stepped into the room. "You found where they were sold?"

"I did!" Tom cleared his throat and lowered his voice. "Yeah. I mean, yes, I did."

"Where?"

"A little convenience store in Worcester, Massachusetts. It's about an hour from Norwich. Not too much of a drive," Tom answered.

"And they were all sold there?" Stan asked.

"Not only that, they were all bought on the same day, Stan," Tom said. "Every one of them."

"Can you give me an exact location?" he asked.

Tom nodded. "Oh yeah. Street address, owner's name. All that good stuff. They were paid for with cash."

"That does not matter," Stan stated. "If it was paid for with cash, there is a good chance the business is close to where Ezra is located. Whoever purchased the phones, either Pettigrew or one of his subordinates, would probably pass by this store on a regular basis. Especially if it is a small corner store. Otherwise, they would have purchased the phones at a larger establishment."

"You think so?" Tom asked, glancing back at the screen.

Stan nodded. "While Pettigrew and his team are good at covering some of their tracks, they are not skilled in thinking like criminals. At least not yet. They are rough in their planning. Yes, they used cash, but instead of spreading the purchases out over different areas and in different towns, all the phones were bought in the same store. That is a mistake. A mistake I hope to capitalize on."

"When are you going up to Worcester?" Tom asked.

"After breakfast," Stan answered. "I will call for a ride now. By the time it arrives, I will be ready. If I am fortunate, I will locate them this evening."

"Are you staying in the city tonight, then?"

"Will that be a problem?" Stan asked.

Tom shook his head, chuckling. "No. It won't be a problem. I'm just wondering. I don't want to have everything locked up and you unable to get in."

"Ah," Stan nodded. "I appreciate your concern. No, I will rent a hotel room. Or find a place to sleep. But you need not worry about me. Would you like me to return to inform you as to the results of the situation?"

"That depends," Tom replied. "If you end up engaging in some extreme violence, probably not. Not to be that person, but I don't want that tracking back to me."

"I am not offended," Stan assured him. "I understand completely, and I will endeavor to keep you free from any ill effects of my actions. Tom, I cannot thank you enough."

Tom felt his face redden. "I'm happy to do it, Stan. Really, I am."

"I appreciate how much you have done for me," Stan told him. "I want you to understand that should you need something, please think of me, and I will do my best to help you as you have helped me."

"I understand," Tom told him. "Listen, I'll put on some tea, and we can share another cup before you go. Sound good?"

"Yes," Stan nodded. "It most certainly does."

✳ ✳ ✳

The tea was finished, and the bags were packed. Stan stood outside, waiting for the ride to Worcester to show up. Tom was inside, engaged in an online discussion for one of his classes. Movement on his right caught Stan's attention, and when he looked, he saw Miss walking toward him across the old parking lot.

"You're leaving," she stated.

"I am. I sought you out a short time ago, but I could not find you."

"I was thinking," she told him.

Stan nodded. "It is a good thing to do alone. Sometimes, others cannot keep their thoughts to themselves, and so you are unable to think of your own."

"Will you return?" she asked.

"Not soon," he answered. "But time does not mean much when you are dead, and so I hope you will not feel too keenly the passage of it."

She smiled at him. "I like the way you talk, Mr. Owens."

He inclined his head in thanks. "It is a result of my youth, I am afraid. But I am glad you appreciate it."

"What will you do when you have exacted your revenge?"

"I will return home," Stan answered. "I will tell my friend that his killer has been punished, and I will hope for the recovery of my injured friend."

"Do you think violence will help either of them?" Her tone was neither derisive nor condescending.

"I do not seek violence to bring my dead friend back to life, nor do I seek violence to return my injured friend to health. I seek violence to ensure that the guilty party does not harm anyone else."

"When I was alive," Miss began, "I believed in an afterlife. One in which I would go to a just reward. A place where I could bask in the glow of the Almighty." She looked hard at him. "This was not the case. Not for me."

Stan waited.

"Despite this loss," she continued, "I remain convinced in the principles in which I was raised. It is wrong to seek vengeance, Mr. Owens, and I fear you shall suffer for it."

"Of all the things I have done," Stan told her. "Of all those I will do, the killing of this man will be the least among them. If I am to burn, it will be for actions far worse than those I am about to take."

"I wish you all the best, Mr. Owens," Miss said, turning away from him. "And I hope your death is a quick one."

Stan nodded as she walked out into the field.

"And I wish the same," he murmured and waited for the car to arrive.

CHAPTER 36
WORCESTER, MA

Stan sat on the bench, and if any of those around him looked, it appeared as though he was alone.

He wasn't, of course.

Ray sat beside him. They looked out over the street, at the cars and the pedestrians, the buildings and the occasional scooters.

"How are you?" Stan asked.

"More than a little impressed. Place is strange to me. I mean, I wasn't that familiar with Worcester when I was alive, but I know it sure didn't look like this." The dead man shook his head and chuckled. "Nope, not at all."

"It is larger than I thought it would be," Stan stated.

"Is it?"

He nodded. "Much larger, I am afraid. I believe this will make my task much more difficult."

"Maybe," Ray agreed. "Don't let it get you down, though. You'll find him."

Stan appreciated the dead man's confidence. He did not feel it, but he did appreciate it.

"Do you see her?" Ray asked, pointing.

Stan followed the line of Ray's finger and saw an older woman sitting on another bench on the other side of the park. A younger man stumbled towards her and sat down, passing through her. He shivered, stood up and hurried away.

In silence, Stan watched her. Nearly an hour passed before she stood up, paced several times around the bench, and then sat down again.

She repeated the process half an hour later.

"It seems as though she cannot leave," Stan observed.

"Want I should go and talk with her?" Ray asked.

Stan considered the question for a minute, then nodded. "Please. Do not draw attention to me, if you can help it. Do not try to hide me, though."

"Sure," Ray chuckled.

Stan watched the dead man get to his feet and followed his progress across the park.

The dead woman noticed Ray immediately and stood as he approached. Stan watched, curious, as Ray stopped and spoke with her. The two conversed for some time, and when he returned, he slowed down long enough to say, "Walk behind me to the entrance."

Stan did not ask why. Instead, he got up and, without looking at the dead woman, followed Ray out of the park. When Ray turned left, which would lead them behind a parking garage that would hide them from anyone in the park, the dead man slowed down.

"They're looking for you," Ray told him.

"Who?"

"This Pettigrew guy that you talked about. He is. The lady, Matilda, she told me there about a dozen or so ghosts throughout the city keeping an eye out for you. Guess this guy Pettigrew is paranoid."

"Not so much paranoid as observant," Stan corrected. "He is an intelligent man, one who knows he has created an issue with the death of my friend and the failed attempts to kill me. It would be logical that he would establish outposts. This is a good sign."

"How so?" Ray asked.

"He would not waste a resource if he was not here in the city," Stan explained. "Yes, it shows he was expecting me. However, it also shows he is here and creating some sort of barricade, a way for him to survive an encounter with me."

"Will he?" Ray asked.

"I am hopeful he will not," Stan answered. "I want the man dead for what he has done, and I hope to see him that way."

"She said they're supposed to report any sighting of you."

"Does she know what I look like?" Stan asked.

Ray chuckled. "She told me they showed her a picture, but her eyesight is just as bad as when she died. And she didn't have her glasses on. She can't see anything past five feet, but she didn't tell them that."

Stan nodded. "I doubt I will be so fortunate with others who have been left to look for me. Now, I will need to look out for the dead and for where Pettigrew is hiding."

"Think it'll take a while?"

"Yes," Stan said. "Longer than I would like. Come, let us find a place to rest for a while. I would prefer to hunt more in the dark."

"Why?" Ray asked.

"Because it will be easier to avoid the dead," Stan answered and started down the alley.

✳ ✳ ✳

"Getting the feeling that he left the Norwich area," Big Mike said.

Robert shifted the phone from one ear to the other. "No one has seen anything?"

"Not a sign. And it's not like the past week or so. There were sightings of him just about everywhere. And now, not a thing."

An uncomfortable feeling crawled up Robert's back. "Do you think he's left the area for good?"

Big Mike paused, then answered, "Yeah. I think he's gone. I'd keep an eye out for him. He's not your regular guy; in case you haven't figured that out on your own yet."

"No," Robert sighed. "I had. Thank you, Big Mike. I appreciate it."

"Not a problem. Say hey to your boss for me."

"Will do," Robert answered. He ended the call and then sent a quick text to Mr. Pettigrew.

Big Mike thinks our friend is out of town. I would surmise he's headed here.

Robert held the phone in his hand as he waited for Mr. Pettigrew's response. It came a few moments later.

Make sure to get the office ready for our friend. Ask around town to see if anyone has seen him. You know how distracted he gets.

Robert sent back a thumbs-up emoji and gathered his belongings. He would need to go out into the city, and the days were getting colder.

CHAPTER 37
GHOSTS AND A STORY

Tom lay on his stomach, eyes closed and his breathing coming in long, easy breaths. Lisbeth's fingers worked on the knots in his shoulders, breaking them up and releasing the tension that had been building for years.

"How are you feeling?" Lisbeth asked.

Tom groaned in response, and she laughed.

"Good," she said and kissed the back of his head. "I did massage work for a little bit, so there's not much for me to compare this to, but your back is the tensest I've ever worked on."

"I'm sorry."

"It's okay," she told him. She paused and then added, "You have a lot of scars."

"Rough times," he admitted. "Most of them are old, though."

"Still, you shouldn't have so many."

He tried to shrug, but his shoulders felt too good, and the effort failed. "Do you have scars?"

"A few," she answered, moving her hands down to the center of his back. "Except mine are from normal things."

"Normal things?" he asked, grinning. "What are those?"

"Falling down, falling off a bike. Scrapes. You know, things like that."

"I have some of those," Tom told her.

"What about this one?" she asked, tracing a long scar down one shoulder blade.

Tom frowned, tried to imagine which one she meant, and then

laughed. "Oh, that was a piece of glass when a room collapsed on me."

"What?"

He nodded. "Yeah, my dad and I were in this ranch house in western Massachusetts, and the bedroom we were in collapsed. I was near the window, which was good and bad. Good, because I was able to get out. Bad because the glass snapped in."

"That's terrible," she murmured.

"Yeah, it wasn't a lot of fun when it happened," he admitted. "But we were both okay. Scratches and bruises. Nothing broken."

"How many stitches did it take?"

"Thirty," he told her.

"Do you have a lot of scars like that?"

"Like what?"

"From incidents with ghosts?" She kissed the scar, and he shuddered with pleasure.

"Most of them are from incidents with ghosts. Couldn't be helped. Dad and I were really trying to help as many people as we could." Tom opened one eye and saw her looking down at him. "You don't have to feel sorry or anything. We needed to get the ghosts out of the houses. In some cases, they were hurting people."

Lisbeth nodded but didn't say anything else.

"We did that a lot," Tom continued after a moment. "Probably more than we should have. You know, I look back at what happened, to the different times each of us was hurt, and I wonder if something there helped to speed up his Alzheimer's. More than the last incident, you know?"

Her fingers worked on his lower back. "You haven't told me anything about the last incident, Tom."

"I'm sorry."

"You don't have to be sorry," she said, her voice soft. "You don't have to tell me the story, either. I was just letting you know."

Tom swallowed, felt the tension rise and forced it back down.

"Not too long ago," Tom began, "we went up to a friend's house. There are a lot of ghosts there. Not like here, where everyone is secured and set aside. The ghosts in the friend's house, they wander. They're more roommates than anything else. But one of them was losing her mind and no one really knew it. Nobody knew why. She focused her anger on my dad. Again, no reason why. Everyone thought it would be okay, though. That if she was kept away from him, that would be fine."

Tom cleared his throat. "Maybe it would have been. I don't know. What I do know, though, is that she didn't stay away. She found him, and she attacked him. She blinded him, Lisbeth. And I think that's what really did him in."

Tears welled up, and Tom let them fall. Lisbeth leaned forward and lay upon him. Her weight was comforting, as was her warmth.

"It's okay to cry," she whispered in his ear. "It's okay to be sad. I'm here, Tom, and I don't think I'm going anywhere."

She kissed the back of his head, and they lay together in silence.

CHAPTER 38

WELL-SPOTTED

For two days, Stan had avoided the dead scattered around the city of Worcester. He and Ray found them in strategic places, at the corners of main thoroughfares and busy intersections. And so, he and Ray had begun avoiding those parts of the city.

Worcester, like any city, had plenty of ways to get around, and Stan had no fear of cities.

On the morning of the third day, Stan spotted a man he knew to be one of Pettigrew's.

Stan had been sitting beneath a tree, watching the city come slowly to life when the man had come out of a parking garage. Stan recognized him from Mason, too. Once Pettigrew's employee had gone a short distance, Stan stood up and followed.

It was not a difficult task.

The man did not suspect anything, and so he acted accordingly. The man walked leisurely, and stopped at the same convenience store the phones had been purchased from. Stan lingered a short distance away, and when the man came out of the store, he carried a newspaper and a cup of coffee.

Stan continued to follow him, and then, finally, Stan came to a stop. Ahead of him, he saw a dead man standing by a building. A moment later, Pettigrew's man entered the building, and through the glass door, Stan could see him stop in front of a security station. The man passed the paper to the security guard and then stepped out of view.

Stan walked back a short distance and brought out Ray's medal. The ghost appeared a heartbeat later.

"Mornin'," Ray grinned. "Looks like a good day."

"It is tolerable so far," Stan confirmed. "I have a question for you."

"Sure."

"Would you do me the kindness of going into the building directly across from here?" Stan pointed out the building.

"Sure. How come?"

"One of Pettigrew's men entered it," Stan replied. "I am hopeful you might see exactly where he has gone and whether or not Pettigrew is in the structure."

"Yeah," Ray nodded. "I can do that. Give me a couple of minutes, okay?"

"Of course," Stan said, and he leaned back against the building.

Time passed slowly, and nearly fifteen minutes passed before Ray returned, a frown on his face.

"What is wrong?" Stan asked.

"I can't get in," Ray grumbled. "That's what's wrong. No matter how I tried, I couldn't get in. Not through the front door, not through the back. Not through the walls or the windows. Something kept pushing me away. I tried talking to the ghosts around the building, but they didn't speak any English, and I don't speak any of whatever they were speaking."

"There is more than one ghost?"

"Oh sure," Ray nodded. "Got to be four or five of 'em. And those are the ones I saw. I think there might be more, but I'm not sure. I was getting kind of angry. Looks like they don't want ghosts going in there."

"But they want people," Stan replied. "I saw the man enter."

"Oh, sure. There's a few living people in there." Ray glanced over his shoulder at the building. "I saw the security guard, he's in there reading a paper. A couple of others, I could see them through their windows, you know?"

"Did anything happen when you were close to the windows?"

"Like what?" Ray asked.

"Did you notice anything with the electronics?" Stan clarified. "Were you affecting the machines in any sort of way? Were the lights flickering?"

"Nope. Not a thing was out of the ordinary. It was strange."

Stan frowned. "Perhaps they have established a protective field against the dead."

"Because of you?"

"There is a possibility," Stan confirmed. "This strengthening of the building concerns me, however. If they have prepared against an attack from the dead, how are the defenses against the living? Pettigrew has already shown he is unafraid to use violence. Will he be so brazen as to use it here, too?"

"Got me," Ray said, grinning. "I have no idea what you're talking about. But if you need someone to stand next to you and fight, hell, I'll be happy to do that."

Stan nodded in appreciation. "I may need to take you up on that offer."

"What now?"

"Now, I find an establishment where I might order something palatable," Stan answered. "It has been some time since I have eaten."

CHAPTER 39

WORRIES, FEARS, AND BASE SUSPICIONS

Anxiety washed over him.

Ezra could not shake the feeling that something was going to go wrong. And catastrophically so.

He was not, and had never been, someone to give any credence to bad omens or premonitions of disaster. Yet the sense that his efforts at eliminating Stan Owens would fail threatened to overwhelm him.

With a shake of his head, Ezra got out of his chair, walked into the bathroom and took a quick shower. He no longer went home at night. One of the safety features of the office building was the presence of a large apartment on the top floor. It was accessible only by the elevator, and he felt protected within the apartment. The windows were double the thickness, the electrical lines were protected from the dead, and his isolation would sever as a defense against Stan Owens, should the man breach the security of the business.

And that was a fear.

Ezra knew Owens could handle his own in a fight. The number of bodies left behind was a blunt statement in that regard. The discovery of the two most recent bodies in the woods in Connecticut, where it looked as though the men had engaged in a murder/suicide, showed Owens' adeptness at staging a scene.

Could that, he wondered, translate into successfully breaking into the building and bypassing not only the security he had established with the dead but the flesh and blood security, too?

Ezra shuddered, turned off the water and towel dried. Within a short time, he was on his way to the office floor in the elevator. When the doors opened, he saw Robert unlocking the office door.

"Good morning, sir," Robert greeted, smiling.

Ezra managed a small grin. "Good morning yourself, Robert. Safe drive in?"

"It was, thank you." Robert held the door open. "I picked up the paper for Carlos. He took that extra shift last night so we wouldn't be unprotected."

"Did he now?" Ezra asked.

"He did."

The two men entered the office, and Robert lingered to one side, closing and locking the door after Ezra took a seat in the small foyer. He remained sitting in silence as Robert went about the morning routine. The man started coffee for Ezra, turned on the computer and the office lights, and then looked at the mail that had come through later in the afternoon.

"No more word on Owens?" Ezra asked.

"No, sir," Robert answered. "Not yet. As soon as he's spotted, we'll know. And I'm scheduled to go out among the dead today to try and gather some information. We're also due to get a check-in from Abigail. Things seem to be going well for her."

Ezra nodded his agreement. "I can't stress enough how I appreciate both of you, Robert."

"We know that, sir," Robert chuckled. "It's one of the reasons why we're happy to help you. You always treat us well. Not too many bosses would do that."

Ezra smiled. He understood the sentiment, when he was younger, he had worked under several managers who were less than impressive when it came to employee welfare and morale. Ezra remembered those men well, and he distinctly remembered how angry those men had left him feeling.

"I recognize good help, Robert," Ezra stated, accepting a cup of coffee from him. "You and Abigail both are not only good help, but you are fine people. I appreciate all you do. When will Abigail call?"

Robert shook his head. "I expect she'll check in soon enough. Probably after I return from my rounds on the sentries."

"Make sure you're safe when you do so," Ezra warned. "No one seems to know where Stan Owens is, and I have the sinking feeling he's already here."

Robert frowned. "That would be entirely disagreeable, sir. I hope someone sees him soon. Maybe out in Norwich or back in Mason, New Hampshire."

Ezra nodded his agreement. "It would be some of the finest news ever if we learned he was far, far from us."

"Agreed, sir."

Silence slipped over them as they drank their coffee, and Ezra tried to shake the feeling that Owens was waiting outside the office door.

Robert strolled along the sidewalk, smiling at those he passed and enjoying the warmth of the late morning sun. He was nearly halfway through the sentries, and all had been well so far. Each ghost had been where they were supposed to be, and the report from each had essentially been the same.

No sign of Stan Owens.

It was a pleasant report to receive. Robert had seen the videos of Owens fighting. He had witnessed the interaction with the ghost in the woods of Connecticut, and while he would not say so to Mr. Pettigrew, Robert was terrified.

There was no scenario where he or Mr. Pettigrew would come out on top in a confrontation with Owens. There was too much power in the man. Too much risk for them.

Robert entered the foyer of a small, rundown movie theater and used a key to let himself in. He walked to the manager's office, used a second key to open that door, and then stepped into the room. He shivered at the chill and waited. Several minutes passed before a shape took form in front of him.

In a moment, Robert faced a demure-looking woman who hid beneath a large shawl. Her face, pale and pinched, gave no hint as to her age. He could not see the cause of her death, and for that, he was thankful.

Others were gruesome and left him shaken.

"Mrs. Keen," he greeted, nodding to her. "How are you this morning?"

"I am doing quite well, thank you," she smiled. "I do have news for you."

Robert straightened up. "Do you?"

She nodded. "I do. I saw that man you asked me to look for. Not once, but twice, in fact."

"When was this?" Robert asked, taking his notepad and pen out from his back pocket.

She tapped the tip of her nose with her index finger, frowned and then smiled. "Oh yes. The first time was this morning."

Robert jotted down the information and then looked at her. "This morning? Are you sure that wasn't the second time?"

"I'm quite sure," Mrs. Keen laughed. "I don't have much to do in this little place except watch people walk by. Your gentleman's face is recognizable, so that's how I know it was this morning."

"Alright, so it was this morning." He underlined the information and looked back up. "And when was the second time?"

"Just a minute ago."

Robert did his best to hide how disappointed he was with where the conversation was heading. "A minute ago?"

She nodded and pointed out the room's solitary window. "You can see him now. He's standing just inside the mouth of that alley."

Robert glanced out the window to humor her but stiffened as he realized she was telling the truth.

Stan Owens stood across the street, half hidden in the alley.

And he was staring at the theater. The man knew Robert was inside.

"Does he owe you anything?" Mrs. Keen asked politely. "Is that why you're looking for him?"

Robert shook his head, murmuring, "Not really, no. We do have a surprise for him, and we don't want it spoiled by him coming to work too early."

"That's terribly nice of you, young man." She beamed at him. "I hope you have a wonderful celebration."

"So do I," Robert agreed.

"You'll let me know how it goes?"

"I will be most happy to do so," he stated, forcing a smile. "Thank you, Mrs. Keen, you've been exceptionally helpful."

The old woman smiled proudly at him, and Robert walked to the foyer. He took several deep breaths to get himself under control and then left the safety of the theater. Robert made every effort to appear as though nothing was wrong, that fear was not crawling up his spine or churning his guts.

He was surprised when he took his phone out of his pocket and discovered his hand wasn't shaking.

Whistling to himself, he brought up a rideshare app, punched in the location for a pharmacy he had passed half a block up, and started to walk toward it. He fought to keep his steps steady and his eyes straight. He wanted nothing more than to look back to see if Stan Owens was following him.

But he didn't need to look back to know the man was.

Owens was hunting them down, and sooner rather than later, he would find them.

If he hadn't done so already.

CHAPTER 40
FLUSHED OUT

Stan watched Pettigrew's man get into a car and leave. He had no doubt the man would return directly to Pettigrew to inform him that Stan had found the right city.

It had been a simple matter to allow himself to be seen by one of the dead sentinels, and he had been sure to be seen by one who was well within a mile radius of the building Stan had seen Pettigrew's man enter.

Ray remained near the building, his medal hidden.

With any luck, Pettigrew's man would return to the building, and it would be where Stan could find Pettigrew as well.

Clasping his hands behind his back, Stan walked along the sidewalk. He would return to where he had hidden Ray's medal and collect it. Then, in a place where privacy could be assured, he and the dead man would speak.

He hoped Pettigrew's man would go to the building.

"You saw him?" Ezra asked and hated the sickening sensation in his stomach.

Robert nodded, his hand shaking as he poured himself a cup of coffee.

"Sit down," Ezra said, keeping his voice steady.

"Thank you, sir," Robert murmured and sat down, his hands wrapped around the coffee mug. "I shouldn't react like this. I'm a grown man."

"And he is a killer," Ezra replied. "Your reaction is quite understandable, Robert. Do not think less of yourself for being upset. I'm agitated as well."

Robert looked up in surprise. "You're certainly not showing it, sir."

Ezra chuckled and sat down in his own seat. "Well, I'm feeling it, Robert. More than I would like to admit. So, tell me again, what did Mrs. Keen say?"

"She told me she had seen Stan this morning," Robert began. "And that she had seen him just a few minutes before and that he was there, too."

"And he was there. Across the road?"

Robert nodded. "I could see him, and he was looking at the theater."

Ezra frowned. "You could see him?"

"Yes." Robert took a sip of coffee. "He was half in and half out of a shadow in an alley. I think he was trying to hide."

"No," Ezra answered. "He wasn't. He was trying to spook you into running."

Robert paled. "And I did."

"But you took a Lyft here, correct?" Ezra asked, sensing the panic rising in Robert.

"Yes."

"Did you see Stan at all while you were waiting?" Ezra asked.

"I watched him almost the entire time. He was still in the alley when I got in the car. In fact, he was still there as we pulled away."

Ezra smiled with relief. "That means he didn't follow you."

Robert sagged into his chair and nearly spilled his coffee. "You're right. He wasn't near a car, and there was an accident right behind us when we drove through the Elm Street intersection. If he were following, he would have been trapped in the traffic jam."

"I don't think he was following," Ezra smiled. "As disconcerting as this has been, it shows that our sentinel system works, Robert. And it has alerted us that Owens is here in the city. I will most assuredly be reaching out to Big Mike for some additional assistance with physical security."

"Extra security would be good," Robert nodded. "Anything would be, I think."

"Agreed," Ezra smiled and picked up his phone.

✳ ✳ ✳

Stan had found an abandoned building and a way into it the night before, and he had made himself comfortable on the second floor. It was a block from the building Pettigrew's man had entered, not once, but twice.

Ray's medal lay on the floor beside him, the ghost keeping watch on Pettigrew's place once more. Stan, wrapped in blankets he had purchased from an Army surplus store, chewed on a bit of beef jerky, contemplating on when might be best to attempt an assault on Pettigrew.

His cell phone began to ring, and he looked at it with surprise for a moment. When he saw Gwen's name appear, he picked it up and answered the call.

"Gwen," he said, smiling. "How are you?"

"I'm okay, Stan," she responded, and he heard a hesitation in her voice.

"What is wrong?" he asked. "Are you ill? Do you need me to return to New Hampshire?"

"I'll always need you, Stan," Gwen answered. "But I called to tell you that Adam died."

Stan's shoulders sagged. "He passed?"

"He did, just an hour ago. I would have called sooner, but I was with a client," she said. "I'm sorry."

"I am sorry as well," Stan said, his voice thick. "He was a good man and a good friend. I will miss his company. Have any funeral arrangements been made yet?"

"Not that I know of."

"I will make them, then. I will call the hospital shortly and make sure they know this. I do not want him going unclaimed," Stan stated.

"That won't happen," Gwen replied. "I won't let it."

"Thank you."

They were silent for a moment, and then Gwen asked, "When are you coming home?"

"Soon, I hope," he responded. "I believe I am nearly done here. When that is the case, I will return home to be with you, to drink tea with you, and forget the world as much as I can."

"That would be nice. I miss you terribly," she said.

"I miss you, too."

They talked for a short time longer, Gwen mentioning some of the idiosyncrasies of her clients, if not their names. She told him of the happenings in Mason, and about the people. Everyone, except Adam, of course, seemed to be doing well.

"When it's time," Gwen told him, "you should fly home."

"I am only two hours away," he reminded her.

"I know. But flying makes it seem faster, don't you think?"

"I am not sure," he admitted. "Perhaps it does."

"I love you," she laughed and then went quiet as though she had said too much.

"I love you, too," Stan replied. "And this is a new feeling for me. I enjoy it. I would like to see where we can go with it if you are amicable to the idea."

Gwen laughed again. "Yes, I think I'm amicable to the idea, Stan."

Smiling, he listened as she told him again about how much she missed him.

CHAPTER 41

BIG MIKE'S BIG HELP

The second time Ezra called Big Mike's, the phone was answered by a woman he didn't know.

"May I speak with Big Mike, please?" he asked.

"Who's this?" Her voice, both high and nasal, punched through the phone.

"This is Ezra Pettigrew."

"Ezra? What—" she stopped, and on the other end, he heard a second voice. "Oh. Okay. Yeah, I'll bring the phone to him. Hold on."

He heard the heels of her shoes click across the floor, then the knock of a fist on a door, and Big Mike's grumbling call for her to enter. Their conversation was difficult to hear, and Ezra suspected she had covered the mouthpiece with her hand.

"Ezra," Big Mike said a moment later. "What can I do you for?"

"I was looking to hire some more help," Ezra answered. "Someone a little physical."

"What for?"

"My place of business," Ezra told him. "I'm expecting trouble to show up soon, and I'd like to have a couple more guys who don't mind doing dirty work."

"You need 'em to be subtle?"

Ezra considered the question a moment before answering. "No. Not at all. I need this problem taken care of, and I don't mind if it's a bit messy."

Big Mike chuckled. "There you go. That's the attitude you need if you're going to make life easy for yourself. Yeah, I got a couple guys I can send your way. Give me the address and I can have them there tomorrow morning."

"I'll pay double if you can have them here tonight," Ezra stated.

"That bad?"

"Yes," Ezra said, clearing his throat.

"Hell, you don't have to pay double. I'll have 'em over tonight. Just give me that address."

Ezra did, thanked the man for his consideration, and ended the call.

He needed the men to be here as soon as they could. He didn't know when Stan Owens would figure out where he was, but he didn't want to risk anything, let alone his own safety.

The call had ended hours before, and Stan lay on his back, eyes closed, and fingers interlocked over his chest. He tried to sleep, but it eluded him.

Adam was dead.

He knew it would be the most likely outcome, especially after the conversation with the dead boy at the hospital, but Stan had hoped it wouldn't be. Adam had been true, a man who had faced his fears and stood by Stan.

And now he was dead. Killed because Ezra Pettigrew had wanted to turn a profit and did not care what he did to obtain it.

Stan shifted his position slightly and wondered if he could get into the building during the night. He doubted it. Ray had given him excellent information regarding the security arrangements and the number of people moving in and out of the structure.

And Adam was dead.

Stan closed his eyes and tried to push the thought away. He did not try to hide from it, nor did he wish to smother it within the recesses of his thoughts. He simply could not focus on the knowledge of his friend's death at the forefront of each idea that came forth.

Stan knew it would interfere with any plans he attempted to make. He knew, too, that it would cause him no small amount of trouble when he sought to enact the plan. It would not serve to be distracted when entering the building. A mistake against a ghost would be acceptable. The iron still embedded in him would serve as his armor and protect him from all but the gravest of mistakes.

Foolishness against a human was something else. A man or woman armed with a pistol, even something as small as a .22, like the pistols the men in Connecticut had, could be fatal.

And Stan had no desire to die. He wanted to avenge his friend's death, punish Pettigrew for the offenses the man had committed, and then return to Mason.

For the first time in his life, Stan found himself wanting the comfort of another person. Specifically, the comfort of a woman.

The abuse he had survived at the hands of his granduncle had crushed any desire for intimacy.

Gwen had changed that.

Stan opened his eyes and picked up his phone. He thumbed open the screen and found the photo Gwen had sent him. In the picture, she sat in her small office at home, a cup of coffee in one hand and the other resting on her thigh. She wore a long, flowing black skirt that hid all but the tops of her black shoes. Her sweater, black and overly large, hung off one shoulder, revealing the pale, smooth flesh whose touch he could remember with painful clarity.

Stan looked at the image a moment longer, then set the phone down and closed his eyes once more. With Gwen's image firmly fixed in his mind's eye, sleep crept up and claimed him.

Two men had responded to Big Mike's request, and they stood in the small security office of the building. Both grinned at Ezra, their smiles, false and predatory, were highlighted by missing teeth and bad dental hygiene.

Ezra didn't care about that, though. He cared about how violent they were. Whether or not they could handle Stan Owens.

"You want him dead?" Paulo, the shorter of the two, asked, tapping his breast pocket where a printed image of Stan Owens now waited.

"I do," Ezra nodded. "I don't care how you do it. Or where you do it. I want him dead, and then I want his body to disappear, if at all possible."

"Anything's possible," Jerry, the second man, remarked. "How do you want confirmation?"

"I want his head," Ezra snapped, then stopped, surprised at the vehemence with which he had spoken.

Jerry and Paulo burst out laughing, nodding their heads.

"Yeah," Paulo grinned. "We can do that."

"Hell, we can have it pickled for you, too, if you really want," Jerry laughed. "See, this is the type of stuff we like to work with."

"Right?" Paulo shook his head. "We get tired of the, Oh no, my wife is cheating. Go beat up her boyfriend."

"Garbage work, man," Jerry told Ezra. "This, though? Hunting a man down and taking his head off? Yeah, that's the real deal right there. No doubt."

Ezra let out a nervous chuckle. "I'm sorry for my outburst. This man, however, has really become a thorn in my side. I would like him removed as quickly as possible."

"We've got his picture," Paulo said, patting the pocket again. "You don't have to worry about it. We'll take care of him."

"You said he's in the city, right?" Jerry asked.

"Yes. And close by, too," Ezra told them.

"Yeah, we'll get it done," Paulo said, nodding. "We got it."

"When will you check in?" Ezra asked.

Paulo grinned. "No check-ins, Miho. Next time you see us, we'll have the man's head, and we'll collect the rest of our payment. But you don't worry about a thing. We got this."

"Okay then," Ezra nodded.

Each man fist-bumped Ezra, which he returned awkwardly, drawing forth a snicker from the men as they left the building. He locked and secured the door behind them and then retreated to his top-floor apartment.

With any luck, the men would find Owens before the end of the following day, and he could focus clearly on his next business endeavor.

Pausing at his desk, he jotted down several notes about reaching out to his contact in Los Angeles. He would need to establish a recruiting center there.

The plans for the center would serve as a distraction, and he let himself think of them as he climbed into his bed.

CHAPTER 42
ENRAGED WITH THE LIVING AND THE DEAD

Stan woke up angry.

Angry, and what was worse, feeling as though he wasn't able to control it.

He knew he should go and check into a hotel or motel, get himself a warm shower and at least a halfway decent meal. He wouldn't mind a respectable cup of tea, either.

But the thought of those things and the knowledge that he couldn't enjoy them yet further aggravated him. He had no doubt Ezra Pettigrew would be watching all such places. And, if Pettigrew kept true to form, he would have hired more men to replace those Stan had killed.

The memory of the killings sent a thrill through him, and he found himself wanting to stumble upon some of those men. He had no compulsion about visiting violence upon men such as those. Stan closed his eyes and took several breaths, trying to calm himself. He would need to leave the safety of the abandoned building, and it would not do for him to be enraged when he did so.

After nearly half an hour, he felt prepared enough to leave.

He exited the building cautiously, keeping to shadows and darkened doorways. The night slipped over the city, streetlamps cast their yellow light upon the pavement, and lights of varying colors illuminated the buildings around him.

While he took some comfort in the city, Stan knew it was only due to the noise and the number of people. The city offered him sanctuary far more than it did Pettigrew now. Where Pettigrew had been hidden, and

Stan forced into the open, Stan could now remain hidden.

There was a chance, he knew, of being identified, of being attacked again.

But he was willing to risk it. He needed to get to Ray and speak with the dead man. He wanted to know what was going on with the building, and the ghost had proven to be reliable.

Despite the urge to go directly to Pettigrew's office, Stan started on a long and convoluted path. This was not Mason, New Hampshire. No one would warn him if a stranger came near with ill intent.

And in this city, everyone was a stranger.

Robert fought the exhaustion, threatening to send him back to his apartment. He had an idea, and he needed to act on it. If he went to bed, it might be too late when he woke up.

He fished keys out of his pocket, unlocked the door and entered the small room. He shivered as cold penetrated his flesh, and his breath came out in plumes of white.

"Hello, Spiro?" Robert asked.

A shape materialized a few feet away, the sight of the ghost briefly making Robert nauseous. The man, perhaps in his late forties, didn't have a stomach. Or a back, for that matter. His dress shirt and tie were torn and shredded, stained, like his khaki's, with dark red blood. While Robert did not know the exact details of the man's death, he could see it had been unpleasant.

Spiro smiled, swept a lock of black hair off his forehead and nodded. "Hello, Robert. This is an odd time of the day to check on me. What can I do for you?"

"I just wanted to see how you were holding up," Robert lied. "You have a great view of the city from here, and I know that it can be difficult, at times, for a ghost to embrace what they see."

Spiro nodded. "It had been for a short time. I have always had a liking for cars. When the Hudson Hornet came out, it was like a dream. And if I hadn't driven the damned thing so fast, I could have enjoyed it longer. Anyway, it's just been a real pleasure to look at those cars."

Robert smiled. "Would you like to do more than look at them?"

Spiro nodded with an expression of caution. "What would I need to do?"

"Do you remember how I asked if you would be willing to resort to violence?"

"Yes," Spiro answered.

"The question remains. If you agree to use violence on a particular individual, the one we've asked you to look for, I can promise you that you will have free rein wherever you travel. And there are a lot of fantastic cars out there in the world."

Spiro glanced at the windows. "Yes. I've seen that."

Robert let silence fill the room.

After several minutes, Spiro nodded. "Yes. I'll do it. Will you bring me to him?"

Robert shook his head and opened the door. "No. But I'll let you look."

"I'm not trapped in here anymore?" Spiro asked.

"No. Not at all."

"Mind if I check out some cars first?" Spiro took a hesitant step toward the door.

"Look at any car you want. Just keep an eye out for Stan Owens, and when you see him, try to kill him."

"Kill?"

Robert nodded. "Kill him."

"Okay," Spiro shrugged, walking toward the door. "I'll kill him."

"Spiro," Robert called.

The ghost paused.

"That was a very quick change of heart," Robert remarked, unsure if the dead man was being truthful.

Spiro chuckled. "Didn't have the right motivation before, Robert. I like cars a lot, and I don't know this guy Stan. So, if he dies, I don't care. But I do care about the cars."

Spiro winked, waved and left.

"Are you certain?" Ezra asked, hope surging through him.

Robert nodded. The man looked exhausted and in need of a shower, but there was a tired smile on his face as well. "Yes, sir. I spoke with the ghost a short time ago. I offered him the opportunity to wander freely if he was willing to help us with Owens."

"Why this particular ghost?"

Robert smiled. "He seemed somewhat interested when I first offered it to him. It seems that the world as it is now fascinates him. Specifically, sir, cars. He wants to see more of them, and he knows he can see them with us."

Ezra let out a long sigh of relief. "Let us hope, then, that Spiro is able to accomplish this for us. I don't mind if the men I hired through Big Mike complete the task first or Spiro does. I am more than willing to pay, and regardless of whether or not Spiro succeeds, I am more than happy to have him accompany us on our next business enterprise."

"Here, here, sir."

"Now, you need to go home and shower, Robert. Get clean, sleep late," Ezra continued.

Robert chuckled weakly and shook his head. "Getting clean, yes. Sleeping late? No, I haven't done that for a long time. I don't find it enjoyable. Not since I became a widower."

Ezra nodded. He could not offer sympathy, having never been married. But he could empathize. And Robert was a good man. A loyal one, too. Anyone with either of those qualities was hard to find. With both of them, almost impossible.

✳ ✳ ✳

"You're him."

Stan stopped and looked at the ghost of a man with a hole where his belly should have been.

"I haven't seen this type of Ford before," the ghost told him, gesturing toward a battered black Ford F250 parked close to a building. "I know it's beat-up and all, but it was still worth a look."

"You were sent to look for me by Ezra Pettigrew?" Stan asked, glancing around the narrow and cramped street. He did not see any other ghosts or living people.

"No. Not directly," the ghost replied, brushing a stray lock of hair off his forehead. "Someone named Robert talked me into it. Hell, it wasn't hard, not after I realized I could get to look at cars when I was done with you. I always loved cars, you know?"

"I do not," Stan replied. He unbuttoned his suitcoat, folded it and laid it on a nearby box. "What is it you are tasked with?"

"I need to kill you," the ghost replied. "No offense meant."

"There is none taken," Stan assured him. He removed his cufflinks and set them atop his suitcoat.

"Hey," the ghost chuckled. "You planning on stripping down right here?"

"No. Not at all," Stan answered. He rolled his sleeves up and faced the dead man again. "What is your name, if I may ask?"

"It's Spiro," the ghost answered. "You're kind of an odd duck, huh?"

"I have been referred to as such, yes."

"So," Spiro smiled. "You ready? I can't promise it'll be quick because I don't know what I'm doing."

"That is quite fine, Spiro," Stan replied. "I do know what I'm doing, and I have no intention of making this quick. You will suffer, and you will suffer as much as I can make you in an effort to impress upon your employer that a poor decision was made by sending you after me."

Spiro frowned. "Are you crazy?"

"At times, I worry that I am, yes. Why do you ask?"

"You can't fight a ghost!" Spiro laughed. "Come on, buddy! That's just crazy. I mean, look!"

The ghost stuck his hand in and out of the building.

"If brick doesn't hurt, then what do you have that will, huh?" Spiro shook his head, chuckling. "I mean, as far as I know, salt is the only thing that can keep me contained. That's how I was sent here, in a bag of salt. And it's how they kept me in my room. At least until they opened the door for me."

"You are nearby, then?" Stan asked.

Spiro grinned and gestured toward a building at the end of the street. "That one, right there. See the half tower that comes out? That's where I was. Plenty of windows to look out of. Lots of cars to look at. It was good, but not nearly as good as actually being down on the ground and pocking around them."

"Iron."

The ghost frowned. "What?"

"Iron," Stan repeated. "Iron, salt, lead. There are other items and ways to fend off ghosts, but those three are the most easily accessible to the average person."

"What are you, some sort of professor on ghost stuff?" Spiro asked, grinning. "That's some curious tidbits to have rattling around in the old noggin."

"It is useful information," Stan told him. "I have known it for some time. It will not be useful to you, however."

"And why's that?"

"Because I am going to destroy you," Stan informed the dead man. "And when I am finished, I will make my way into Pettigrew's building, and I will kill him, too."

Spiro shook his head. "You are definitely crazy. Bats in the belfry, buddy. You should have checked into an asylum a long, long time ago." Cocking his head to one side, Spiro grinned. "You sure you want to die tonight?"

"I want to die every night," Stan answered and stepped toward the ghost.

Spiro shrugged and sprang forward, making a ridiculous face as he reached for Stan.

Stan planted his feet, took the initial impact of the ghost's force slamming into him, and then felt that same force vanish along with Spiro.

Leaving his coat and cufflinks behind, he stepped quickly to the building Spiro had identified as his residence. Or at least where Pettigrew had kept him.

Stan had almost reached the door when the dead man appeared, his expression one of confusion, then shock when he saw how close Stan was.

"I don't know what you did, but I don't think you can do it again," Spiro snapped and swung at Stan.

Without any hesitation, Stan raised his left arm and blocked the blow. The ghost's flesh slipped into his own, connected with the iron, and the dead man disappeared.

Stan entered the building, saw a stairwell and followed it up. As he turned onto the next landing, Spiro stumbled out of a room, caught sight of Stan and staggered back. He grasped at the doorknob, but his hands passed through them.

Stan entered the room and closed the door behind him, trapping Spiro in with him.

"I just wanted to see cars," Spiro said, his voice sinking into a whine as he pressed back against the far wall. On the floor, a plain garden hose had been taped down, and Stan suspected it was filled with salt. A glance at the door showed a draft-stopper that overlapped the hose on either side of it.

"Is that so wrong?" Spiro asked.

Stan fixed his attention on the ghost. "You ask me if it is wrong for you to murder a man to satisfy your curiosity regarding the evolution of automobiles after your death?"

Spiro offered up a weak smile. "You know, it doesn't sound that great. Like not a good excuse at all, but it is. When you get right down to it. It's one of the best excuses around."

"I would disagree with you," Stan replied. "Perhaps only on principle at this point. But I do, in fact, disagree with you."

Stan took a step toward Spiro, and the ghost tried to bolt past him.

Stan snapped his arm out, the ghost passing through it and vanishing.

Spiro reappeared a heartbeat later, a few feet to the right.

"Nothing's going to happen to me," Spiro said, his voice trembling. "You can't do anything. Not really. You're just sending me back to my object."

"Yes," Stan nodded. "I know."

Again, Spiro tried to run, and again Stan stopped him. As soon as the ghost disappeared, Stan stared at the floor. It took him less than a second to see it, a piece of wood slightly off colored from those around it.

"What are you doing?" Spiro demanded.

Stan neither answered nor reacted when the dead man struck him. Instead, he focused on prying up the board and removing what was underneath.

Cold and painful against his palm, Stan opened his hand to look down at Spiro's object, a plastic fob with a Chevy emblem inside it.

"That's mine!" Spiro screamed, but he did not try to hit Stan again.

Stan stood and looked at the ghost.

"It is yours," Stan replied. "This is where you reside. This is where you return to when you encounter my iron. Where do you think you will go when I destroy this?"

Spiro's eyes widened. "You can't destroy it."

"Of course I can," Stan stated. "It is dangerous but easy, too. And the danger is well worth it."

"No," Spiro shook his head violently. "No! I don't want to go! Look at all the cars out there! Listen, listen! I won't do anything to you, I promise!"

Stan frowned. "But you promised Pettigrew that you would. It does not do to lie, Spiro. It means you cannot be trusted at all."

Spiro shrieked as Stan dropped the fob to the floor, raised his foot and brought his heel smashing down.

CHAPTER 43
ON THE WARD

"This can be kind of disturbing," Tom told her.

They sat in Lisbeth's car in the facility's parking lot.

She nodded. "I've heard it can be. I haven't been to visit anyone with Alzheimer's before. This is kind of a stupid question, but do they get it right? When it's on TV or in a movie?"

"Depends on the show and the movie," Tom answered. "For the most part, though, they don't. They can't really capture that sense of desperation. Not only from the family members watching what's going on with their loved one, but what you can see on the faces of the people suffering from Alzheimer's. They know they should remember certain things. Names, dates, faces. But that stuff slips away. They can almost grab a hold of it, but it's elusive."

"That sounds like torture," Lisbeth murmured.

Tom watched her attention shift to the entrance of the building.

"You don't have to go in," he told her, his voice soft. "We can go and eat."

She looked back at him and smiled. "No, I want to see your father, Tom. He's important. I know he's your adoptive father and that you guys became a family pretty late, but he's still a significant part of your life. I want to see that man. Even if it's from a distance."

"Okay," Tom smiled, leaned across the console and kissed her. "Let's go."

They got out of the car and made their way to the front. The man behind the security desk saw Tom and grinned.

"Hey, Tom." The man stood and offered his hand. "How you doin'?"

"Okay, Darnell," Tom answered, shaking the man's hand. "This is my friend Lisbeth."

She raised an eyebrow, and when she shook Darnell's hand, she corrected Tom. "I'm his girl, Darnell. Just want to make sure he knows he can tell people that."

Tom's face flushed, and Darnell let out a deep laugh as he let go of her hand.

"That's a good woman, Tom. You treat her right, or someone else will," he warned.

"He will," Lisbeth assured the man as he returned to his seat. "He's bringing me to meet his dad."

Darnell's expression grew serious. "You best brace yourself today. He's not in the best shape. Call came over the radio for additional help and Terrence went over there. He came back with a busted lip and a broken finger. Everybody forgets your dad knows how to fight."

A heavy weight pressed down on Tom's heart, and he nodded. "Thanks for letting me know."

"I'm sorry, big man," Darnell said. "I really am. Maybe come back another day?"

Lisbeth slipped her arm around Tom's waist. "I'm okay with seeing your dad if you're okay with letting me."

Tom nodded, and Darnell gave a knowing smile.

"You're a good woman, Lisbeth," Darnell stated. "Few good people in this world. Go on in and come on back this way when you're done, let me know if your dad's doing any better."

"I will," Tom assured him.

With her arm still around his waist, Tom led Lisbeth into the foyer and toward the hallway that would take them to the secure wing.

He couldn't move his arms or legs, and his head would only turn slightly to either side.

Victor Daniels arched his back against what felt like a belt across his chest and two more across his thighs and shins, respectively.

They had blindfolded him, too. Trapped him in a dark room where no light entered. Not the slightest hint of a shadow.

He could hear voices around him, but they made no sense. Some spoke in foreign languages. Others whispered nonsensical statements about peanut butter and chocolate. The news broadcast and a song by Frank Sinatra could be heard at the very edges.

Victor did not know who Frank Sinatra was or why he knew it, but he did. In fact, he knew all the words to the song.

"How are you doing, Victor?" a voice asked.

He snapped his head towards the speaker. "Take the damned blindfold off, and I'll tell you."

The speaker hesitated, then spoke in a halting voice, "I can't. I'm not allowed to do that."

"Let me go."

"I can't do that either," the speaker told him. "You hurt yourself earlier, and we need to keep you contained a little bit longer."

Victor opened his mouth, started to speak and then stopped. After a moment, he asked, "Are you going to drug me?"

"No," the speaker sighed. "We're not. You were already given a sedative earlier. We don't want to give you another."

Victor snarled. "You wouldn't have to if you just let me go."

"I know that," the speaker assured him. "In fact, as soon as we're sure the sedative has worn off completely, we'll let you go. You'll be free again."

Victor frowned. "You're not keeping me here?"

"No." The speaker sounded exhausted, as though he'd had the conversation a hundred times before. "We just want to keep you safe until it's time to help you."

"You can help me by letting me out of this!" Victor said, surging against the restraints. He heard the bed beneath him move, and someone muttered off in a corner. He shifted his attention toward the new sound, demanding, "Who else is in here?!"

"Two others," the speaker informed him. "They are waiting to help me release you when you are ready."

Victor swore at the speaker and the silent others.

"I know you're angry," the speaker responded. "I'm sorry."

Victor wanted to swear again, but he held his tongue. Despite his anger, he had a sense he should be calm, that he should try and relax. There was something missing. Some key bit of knowledge that would make everything understandable.

After some moments of silence, the rage surged back, and foul language spilled from his lips.

Tom and Lisbeth sat in his bed, the side table lamp casting a pleasing light across the room. Lisbeth lay in the crook of his good arm, her head against his chest.

"I wish you could have known him when he was healthy," Tom said, breaking the pleasant stillness of the room. "He was brilliant. He knew so much."

She took his hand in both of hers. "I can see it in you, Tom."

He smiled. "Thanks."

"I mean it."

"I know you do," he nodded. "He taught me, he loved me, and he cared for me. He's my dad."

She kissed Tom's hand.

"Did it bother you to see him?" he asked.

"Only in that I know it hurts you to see him that way," she answered.

"I don't want anyone to suffer, but I want you to suffer even less."

He kissed the top of her head, leaned back and closed his eyes. Her skin was warm against his own, and Tom wondered how he had gotten so lucky.

CHAPTER 44
HELP AND HELP AGAIN

"Are you okay?" Gwen asked.

"No," Stan answered. "I am hurt."

"What happened?"

Stan lay down on the bed, his body tense. Beyond the thin walls of the motel room he had rented, he could hear the rumbling of the city.

"I found a ghost controlled by Pettigrew," he told her.

"Did the ghost hurt you?" Gwen's tone was one of worry.

"A little, but that was my fault more than the ghost's," Stan informed her. "I took it upon myself to destroy its item. When it exploded, it threw me across the room and knocked me heavily against the wall. I will be fine soon enough. As for right now, though, I am in poor shape. And, what is more, I am angry. Extremely angry."

"With who?"

"With everyone," he answered. "The dead and the living. I would destroy them both."

"Just the ones you have to?" Gwen asked.

"No," Stan sighed. "Anyone I meet."

"That's not good, Stan."

"No, it is not," he agreed. "I am going to stay in for the rest of the day, and I hope to leave this anger behind. It is what I need to do, but it is not what I want to do. And as we all know, need and want can be two extremely different things."

"Talk to me, Stan," she urged. "Tell me what's going on. I don't need specifics, not if you don't want to give them to me. But I do need the basics. What's going on?"

"Adam is dead."

"Yes," Gwen said. "What can you do about that?"

"Nothing."

"Agreed. What can you do for him?"

"I can help bury him," Stan answered.

"And have you started doing that?" she asked.

"No," he admitted. "I was distracted today."

"You were angry today."

Stan smiled. "You are correct. I was angry today."

"Are you angry now?"

"I am never angry when I talk with you, Gwen," he told her.

She laughed. "Good. Let's talk about Adam's final arrangements, okay?"

"Yes. I do not have a pen or paper with me, though, so it may take me some time to memorize what we discuss."

"Don't worry about that," Gwen replied. "I have a pen and paper. I'll take notes and we can go over them at a later time, okay?"

"Yes."

"Now, where do you want Adam brought to?" she asked.

Stan closed his eyes, thought for a moment, and then stated, "Davis Funeral Home in Nashua."

"Do you have a plot yet?"

"I do not," he told her.

"What cemetery would you prefer to bury him in, if it's available?"

"There is Edgewood Cemetery in Nashua," he answered. "It is a beautiful and calming place. If there are any lots available, I would like to purchase one there. Kenny is also buried in Edgewood. It would be good to be able to visit both of my friends there. Do you think we can try to do this?"

"Of course I do."

Stan paused. "Gwen?"

"Yes?"

"Should I buy flowers?" he asked. "I know there were some at Kenny's funeral, and it was pleasant if that is the right word."

"It is the right word if you feel it is," Gwen assured him. "I wish I was there with you, Stan."

He sighed. "I wish you were here, too. I will be home soon, though. And I will see and hold you again."

"Good."

They were silent for a moment, and then she asked, "Do you want to wait on the funeral until you come home?"

"No," Stan replied. "He should be buried as soon as possible. His parents should be invited, but I do not know if they will attend. He has had little contact with them."

"Okay."

They spoke for a short time longer, and then Gwen needed to leave. She had an appointment with a client who was traveling and had to call in.

Stan set the phone down beside him and tried to keep his thoughts still.

But memories of violence drifted up from the depths of his past and swept away all hope of peace.

Chapter 45
A Growing Fear

Ezra found it impossible to leave the safety of his building.

He did his best to remain away from windows, and he had Robert bring in rolls of brown shipping paper. Robert spent the better part of the day covering the glass, making sure Ezra could move about without being seen.

It did not work on the first floor, not with the security guard there. Too many people might become curious at the sight of it, maybe even try to get in. Stan Owens might try, too.

But with the glass covered, Owens could not shoot at him, and while Owens had never used a rifle before, Ezra did not discount the possibility that the man might, at some point, employ one.

He certainly didn't want to find out the hard way.

"How are you doing, sir?" Robert asked, entering the second-floor conference room.

"As well as I can be," Ezra answered. "I can't shake the feeling that he's going to come in here at any moment."

Ezra did not need to clarify who "he" was. Robert was as concerned about Owens as he was.

"I hope the two additional men will find him," Robert admitted, walking over to the coffee maker and starting it.

Ezra nodded in agreement.

"Abigail checked in, by the way," Robert continued. "She said all is going well. She's even brought in an architect to begin the modifications necessary on the open floor spaces."

Ezra chuckled. "Of course, she has. She's a bright woman."

"That she is," Robert smiled. The coffee pot sputtered and hissed. "Do you think they'll kill him?"

"I think they can if they find him."

"I don't think he's going to hide," Robert said, looking down at the coffee pot.

"No, but I think he'll try to get in when he thinks we're at our weakest," Ezra added.

"Agreed, sir."

Ezra's phone rang, and both men jumped.

With a nervous chuckle, Ezra picked up the cell phone, saw it was Abigail and answered it.

"Abigail, you scared me half to death," he greeted.

"I'm sorry, sir, is this a bad time?" she asked.

"I don't think there's a good time at this point," Ezra answered. "Robert and I were just talking about you, though. He reported you have been seeing some success with the preparations for the buildings."

"I am," she confirmed. "In fact, I was calling to see about the possibility of establishing living facilities for the permanent staff outside of the immediate vicinity of the two main buildings. I don't think it would be conducive to have the staff too close to the workshops and training facilities."

"If you think that's best, Abigail, I trust you."

"Thank you, sir," she replied, and he could hear the pleasure in her voice. "I also have a question. A rather more practical question, I'm afraid."

"What is it?" Ezra asked.

"Considering the amount of biological material that will be discarded, we need to consider installing an incinerator. Burying the material will prove to be time-consuming, and it will occupy land that we may later need to establish another building on," she explained. "And I don't think we should try and rely on a separate company to haul the waste away. Financially, the installation of an incinerator would pay out in the long term."

"Do you think we'll be looking at that much material that we would need one?"

"I do. I did some research into the requirements for a permit and the training to operate a basic incinerator. Both, while an expenditure in the beginning, would prove to return our investment just on a lack of future expenses," she explained.

"Okay, you have sold me on the idea," Ezra answered. "Get some quotes and pick the best one."

"I will. I'm also making sure to keep the jobs split up," she continued. "I don't want any one company getting a lion's share of the work. We're diversifying the labor as much as possible."

"Excellent. Make sure you think of a decent bonus for yourself, Abigail," Ezra ordered.

"Mr. Pettigrew—" she started.

"Abigail, you have more than earned it. In fact, I want you to make certain Robert gets the same as you," he stated. "You both have given a great deal to this project, and I can't thank you enough."

"Yes, sir," she sighed. "But only because you've included Robert."

"That's why I did it, Abigail," he told her, softening his tone. "I know you won't give yourself what you're due, but you will do so for others."

"Yes, sir."

"Now, get some rest and enjoy yourself for a bit. Robert and I will speak with you soon," Ezra assured her.

They said their farewells, and Ezra ended the call. He set the phone down and looked at Robert.

"A bonus, sir?" Robert asked.

"A bonus," Ezra nodded. "Let's drink our coffee before it gets cold, Robert."

In silence, they drank their coffee and sat in comfortable silence.

CHAPTER 46

A POINTED ARGUMENT

"Stan."

Stan opened his eyes and sat up.

Ray stood across the room, a look of relief flickering across the dead man's face. "I was worried I wouldn't be able to wake you up."

"I sleep lightly. What is wrong, Ray?"

"Someone's coming," Ray answered. "I saw them earlier, poking around the alley we were in this morning. Then, a little while ago, I saw him across the street. And now, he's downstairs."

Stan nodded, climbed off the bed and put on his suit coat. He stepped into the bathroom, washed his face, ran his fingers through his hair and then returned to the main part of the motel room. He slipped the key into one pocket, his wallet into another, and asked, "Will you follow me?"

Ray grinned. "Sure. You want me to step in if it looks like you need a hand?"

Stan shook his head. "No, thank you. I will deal with the individual. However, if you would like to make certain any electronics he has does not work properly, I would appreciate that."

"Yup, I can do that."

"Excellent," Stan stated. Then, with a deep breath, he opened the door and left the motel room.

✳ ✳ ✳

It was the right motel.

Paulo grinned, went to move, and then stopped.

The target, Stan Owens, turned toward him.

Paulo didn't freeze, he didn't make eye contact. He continued with exactly what he was doing, and that was scrolling through his TikTok feed.

Owens passed by within arm's reach, and the urge to slip a knife into the man's ribs was difficult for Paulo to resist. But he did resist, and he waited until Owens was well past him before turning around to follow.

Paulo had heard the reports about the man, about how he had beaten down and killed numerous others. He had even watched some of the footage available, and while it was impressive, it wasn't anything either he or Jerry hadn't seen or dealt with before.

Physically, Owens wasn't much. Average size, much older than he thought, and walking with obvious exhaustion. The man looked as though he hadn't had a good night's sleep in years, let alone a day or two.

Paulo decided to follow Owens until he stopped, and when he did, Paulo would reach out to Jerry. They would take Owens together just to make sure they didn't make any mistakes. Paulo didn't care how easy of a mark Owens looked; anyone could be more than they appeared, and Paulo and Jerry were excellent examples of that, as any of a dozen others could testify.

If they could still speak.

Paulo grinned and kept an even, steady pace as he followed the wandering man in front of him.

"He's still following you," Ray informed him. "Should I go and mess with his phone now?"

"No," Stan answered. "Wait until I ambush him. He will most likely attempt to call for someone at that point. I would not want him to be able to summon assistance."

Stan continued on, catching glimpses of the man following him on various reflective surfaces. As the night deepened and the lights from various buildings increased, Stan lost the ability to see his follower.

Within a heartbeat, he made a decision and turned down a side street. He saw an alley ahead of him and, a few steps beyond that, a parked box truck with a pair of flat tires.

Stan lengthened his strides, passed the alley and cut in front of the box truck, stopping as soon as he did so. He would remain there, and the man following him would do one of two things. Either turn into the alley, or he would look in front of the truck.

Stan would react appropriately to either one.

Paulo turned the corner and hesitated.

He couldn't see Owens.

His eyes took in the entirety of the street. A single, disabled box truck, a large alley immediately on the left, another a block ahead on the right, and buildings crowded together. None of the buildings looked as though they were easy to access.

Owens wasn't gone. Of that, Paulo was certain. He was in one of the alleys. The one on the right was too far away. Owens would have had to run, and Paulo would have heard him. Plain and simple.

The only option was the alley on the left.

Paulo took his phone out, opened it, and then frowned as the lights around him flickered. A heartbeat later, the phone died, and he couldn't turn it back on. The flickering stopped, but the phone remained dead.

With a muttered curse, Paulo stuffed the phone back into his pocket and pulled a small knife from its sheath in his back pocket. His parole officer had paid an unexpected visit in the afternoon, and Paulo hadn't been able to recover his pistol.

But Owens wouldn't be a match for him with a knife.

No one was.

With his knife ready, Paulo moved to the alley, every sense heightened and a smile spreading across his face.

*** * ***

Stan saw the man start down the alley with the knife in his hand.

Stan slid his belt out of its loops, wrapped some of the leather around his hand and followed. He let the buckle swing back and forth as he watched the man in front of him advance.

Of all those he had faced thus far, this man knew what he was doing. While the others had simply been armed thugs, this one was a true killer. He knew how to walk, how to move, and, most importantly, how to hold a knife.

If anyone could truly harm Stan, it would be this man.

A single thought of Gwen flitted through his mind, and Stan let it pass. He wanted to see her again, but he needed to destroy Ezra Pettigrew, and this man in front of him was an obstacle to achieving that end.

*** * ***

Paulo was less than halfway down the alley when he realized he had made a mistake.

Chuckling, he turned around and saw Stan Owens behind him. Like in the videos Paulo had seen, Stan held a belt in one hand, an old-school style of knife defense. Owens was skilled with the damned thing, too.

It would be a good fight.

"I got to admit, that was a good play," Paulo said, stretching. "Did you duck into a building?"

"I stood in front of the truck."

Paulo nodded. "Never thought of that. Makes sense, though. You would have been able to attack from whatever side I passed by."

"That is correct."

"I've seen the footage of you with that," Paulo added, gesturing with the knife toward the belt.

"It did not bother you."

Paulo shook his head. "It impressed me. Didn't bother me, though, no. You went against a couple of chumps. Guys didn't even know how to hold a knife properly. Kind of think it'll be different if you fight someone who knows what they're doing."

"Is that you?"

Paulo laughed. "Damned right it is. I'll make it quick, though, okay? I won't make you suffer, although I think that guy Pettigrew wouldn't mind if you did."

"No, he would not mind at all."

"I'm curious," Paulo began.

"Why does he want me dead?"

"Yes."

"He killed my friends, and he knows I want to kill him," Owens answered.

"Ah, got it," Paulo nodded. He grinned at Owens. "No hard feelings?"

"No feelings whatsoever."

"My man!" Paulo chuckled. "That is one cold answer. I'll have to remember it."

Paulo raised his knife, winked, and advanced on Owens. He watched as Owens used his free hand to unbutton his jacket, giving him more freedom of movement, and Paulo admired the simple gesture. Owens wasn't afraid, and Paulo appreciated that.

Owens should have been, but still, it was admirable.

Paulo stepped left, feinted right, and attacked to the left.

Owens didn't fall for the feint. He deflected the attack, brushing it aside easily as he snapped the buckle out, not at Paulo's head, as the videos had shown, but at Paulo's elbow. The heavy buckle connected and sent a piercing pain shooting up into his fingertips and numbing the arm from the elbow down.

Paulo absorbed the pain and attacked again, flicking the tip of the blade toward Owens' face before dropping the weapon down and cutting across the upper left arm.

But Owens didn't flinch.

Instead, he pulled his arm back, turning what would have been a debilitating cut through the bicep into nothing more than a harassing injury that hardly cut through the fabric.

Paulo, however, received a strike to his right rib that cracked at least one, if not more.

He drew in a sharp breath through clenched teeth and attacked again, pressing with more speed and violence. Owens met him with the same. Again, the man blocked the attack, absorbed a punch from Paulo and got in close enough to drive a knee toward Paulo's groin. In the dim light of the alley, he was able to see the knee and shift, grunting in pain as the attack deadened his thigh but saving him from a blow that would have put him down.

In an effort to give himself some breathing space, Paulo reversed his grip and slashed with the blade, an inexpert and desperate move, but one that worked.

The blade cut up and across the chest. The fabric of the man's vest and shirt split open, blood appeared a moment later, and the blade continued up. Any normal man with a sense of self-preservation would have pulled back away from the edge of the weapon, yet Owens did not. He stood his ground, let the blade pass through his cheek and up into his hairline and slammed his forehead into Paulo's.

The headbutt staggered Paulo. Stars exploded in his field of vision, and his legs wobbled beneath him. He tried to bring the knife back down on Owens, but the belt buckle smashed into his hand, shattering his fingers against the hilt of the weapon and causing him to drop it.

The pain was overwhelming. Paulo struggled to maintain his balance, to focus on where the knife could have landed, but another strike from the belt buckle, this one against his chin, drove away all hope of recovering the weapon.

Owens could kill him.

No, Paulo corrected himself, struggling against Owen's onslaught, the man would kill him.

And Paulo didn't want to die.

✳ ✳ ✳

Distantly, Stan felt the pain.

It was sharp, grating, and, at the same time, freeing. The man in front of him would be dead in a matter of minutes, if not sooner.

Stan would kill him, and it would not matter. Not in the least.

Stan didn't mind the pain from the injuries. Nor did he care that the blade had cut across his face. Such were the dangers of fighting. Especially when knife fighting.

The man tried to slip away, and Stan sent the belt buckle out with a snap of the wrist. The metal caught his opponent in the temple and sent him tumbling to his hands and knees. Stan stepped over to him and struck the man in the back of the head, sending him crashing face down into a puddle of liquid filth leaking from a dumpster. As the man struggled to rise, Stan pressed a knee into the man's back and pushed his face fully into the puddle.

The stranger tried to move, but Stan increased the pressure and took hold of the man's head with his free hand. He kicked and tried to buck Stan off, but it was of no use, and soon, he stopped struggling altogether.

Stan waited a few more minutes, then he stood and wavered on his feet. He was losing blood quicker than he had thought. He stumbled to the far end of the alley, took out his phone and called Tom.

✳ ✳ ✳

The phone rang, and Lisbeth answered it.

"Hello?" she asked, her voice thick with sleep.

"I am sorry for waking you," a man stated. "I was wondering if I could speak with Tom if he is awake."

"Tom," she said, and in the dim light of the room, she saw him open his eyes.

"Mm?"

"Phone call," Lisbeth told him.

"Thank you," Tom muttered and accepted the phone from her. Lisbeth yawned and watched as the sleep drained from Tom's face.

He sat up and swore. "Okay. Listen, here's what we do. I want you to stay where you are, or at least close to where you are. I'm going to call a friend."

Lisbeth could hear the man on the other end, but she couldn't make out what he was saying.

"No," Tom answered. "He lives in Worcester. Yes... yes, he will answer my call. He's a good friend. I'll call him and give him your number. His name is Frank. Should you just take the chance and call 911?"

Tom paused, listened, then let out a long sigh. "Okay. If you think it's best not to, then don't. Right... yup, I'll call him now."

He ended the call with the stranger, and Lisbeth watched him start a second.

Several rings sounded, and then she heard another voice, and again, she could not make out what was being said.

"I'm fine, Frank. I promise. Listen, I have a friend who can't go to the hospital or emergency services. Can you go to him?"

Lisbeth heard Frank ask a question.

"I don't know how it happened. As far as I know, it's a knife wound. No bullets." Tom paused. "Yeah, I know my choice of friends is suspect. Look who I'm calling."

Frank's laugh came through the phone loud and clear. A moment later, Tom gave him Stan's phone number. "Let me know when he's good to go, okay?"

Tom sighed again and ended the call. His hand was steady as he handed the phone to her, asking, "Could you put this back on the nightstand, please?"

"Of course," she answered and did exactly that. Lying down beside him and snuggling in close, she asked, "Is your friend okay?"

"Oh, yeah," Tom yawned. "He's a tough guy. In every sense of the word. He'll survive the wound. I just don't want him too weak to carry on with his work."

"What does he do for work?"

"Nothing I want the details on," Tom told her, kissing her. "There are some things best left unsaid."

"Not between us," she murmured and kissed him once more.

CHAPTER 47
JERRY

"He's gone."

Ezra looked up from his desk and saw Jerry standing inside the doorway.

"Who's gone?" Ezra asked.

Jerry came in and sat down uninvited. "Paulo. He's gone."

"Well, did he get lost?"

Jerry snorted. "Not likely. No, this guy of yours, this Stan Owens, he must have gotten the drop on him. It's the only explanation."

"Did you find Paulo's body?"

"No," Jerry answered with a shake of his head. "I was able to track where he had gone, but then the signal died. The phone's gone. Paulo's gone. There are signs of a fight. Some blood and a few other things."

Ezra fought back the anger and worry warring inside him. "What sort of things?"

Jerry reached into his pocket and then dropped a pair of teeth onto the desktop.

Ezra looked at them, cleared his throat and asked, "Where did you find those?"

"In a puddle," Jerry answered. "Figured they were Paulo's. One of 'em has a gold filling, and he only ever had his teeth filled with gold if he was gonna fill 'em at all."

"Do you think the blood was his?" Ezra asked.

"Nope. Paulo was good with a knife. His preferred way to kill somebody. I went by his place today and found his pistol was still hidden.

A neighbor said a PO stopped by. That would have kept Paulo from going out armed."

Ezra frowned. "What's a PO?"

"Parole officer," Jerry replied. "We've both got 'em. Of course, Paulo doesn't have to worry about his anymore."

"How can you be sure he's dead?"

Jerry looked at him for a moment, and Ezra felt certain the man was deciding on whether he should strike him.

Jerry took a deep breath and retrieved a phone from another pocket. He set that on the desk beside the teeth.

"This is his phone," Jerry explained. "It's dead. I don't know why, but it is. I found it under the garbage can. Inside the can were Paulo's socks and underwear."

"Where are the rest of his clothes?" Ezra asked, confused.

"My guess?"

Ezra nodded.

"Your boy Owens stripped Paulo down when he killed him. He left the shoes, pants, shirt and jacket out. Some homeless people are probably wearing them or traded them for stuff they need. They would have seen it as a blessing. Good luck to the cops getting his clothes back."

"But where is he?" Ezra asked.

"I told you," Jerry said. "He's dead. More than likely, Owens hid the body somewhere. And since he knew enough to leave the clothes there and then hauled a naked corpse off into the unknown, we're not going to find him anytime soon."

Ezra rubbed at his temples. "Okay. Alright. So, what happens next? Do you have a recommendation for another person to work with?"

Jerry snorted a laugh. "Hell, no. He was the only one I would ever tackle someone like Owens with. Thing about Paulo, he made rash decisions. This time, it cost him. No, I'm not going after Owens. Money's not worth it. Can't spend it if I'm dead."

Ezra nodded in understanding, hiding the fact that his mind was racing. He would need to find someone else who would kill Owens, but there was still another job Jerry might be able to help him with.

"What about dealing with a woman?" Ezra asked.

Jerry raised an eyebrow. "Deal with how?"

"I need her business," Ezra told him. "I don't need her."

"She anything special?" Jerry asked.

Ezra shook his head. "No. I have an address for you. It's an easy enough job. Nothing like Owens. You would need another man to drive a truck, probably one of the U-Haul box trucks. While her stock isn't large, I don't think a van would be big enough. Is this something you can handle?"

"Sure," Jerry said. "How much money am I losing for dropping Owens?"

"You're not losing any," Ezra smiled. "You'll get paid the same. I see no difference in their worth to me. She's less challenging, that's all."

"Armed?"

"No," Ezra replied. "I have had her investigated, and she is not one to carry weapons. In fact, there's not even a security system in her warehouse. Her office is located there, too."

"So, I go, kill her and have someone load her goods into a U-Haul, and we bring it back to you?"

"That's all you have to do," Ezra confirmed.

"Okay," Jerry nodded. "I can do that. I even have a guy I can work with who has his own box truck. Give me the address, and we'll leave in an hour."

Ezra sighed with pleasure, wrote down the address on a piece of paper from his notepad, and handed it off.

Jerry stood, nodded, tucked the paper into his pocket and left as quietly as he had come.

For a short time, Ezra sat in his chair and looked at the cell phone and the teeth Jerry had left behind. Finally, he stood and went to a filing cabinet. From one of the drawers, he removed a Faraday bag, went back to his desk and placed the three items into the bag, sealing it.

With any luck, Paulo would return as a ghost, and he would be attached to one of the teeth. Ezra didn't believe the phone would be terribly important, but it didn't hurt to take the precaution that it might be.

Smiling, Ezra put the Faraday bag into a desk drawer and went to speak with Robert.

✳ ✳ ✳

Frank Benedict sat in one of his chairs and finished the last suture.

He leaned back, stripped his nitrile gloves off and dumped them into a trash bag between his feet. He looked at Stan Owens, a man who had sat with perfect stillness during the insertion of an IV and then through the cleaning and closing of his knife wound.

All without the benefit of an anesthetic.

Looking at the scars on the man, Frank could understand how Stan had done it.

Someone had tortured the man, and for a long time, if the age of the scars were any clue. Someone had even gone so far as to use him as an ashtray.

The thought turned Frank's stomach, so he set it aside.

"How are you feeling?" Frank asked.

"I am feeling much better knowing that the wound has been so expertly cared for," Stan replied. His speech, clipped and precise, reminded Frank of actors on television pretending to have autism.

He didn't think Stan was pretending.

"I'm going to let those sit for a bit before I clean up any of the blood. I need your body to relax, okay?" Frank asked.

"I understand."

"Are you cold?" Frank stood up and stretched.

"I am not," Stan replied. "However, if my partial nudity is offensive to you, I will happily cover myself."

Frank chuckled and shook his head. "No, it's not that. I'm honestly just worried about whether or not you're cold. If you're not, you can stay exactly as you are. Are you thirsty?"

"I am."

"Is there anything you prefer to drink?" Frank asked. "I don't have much, but I might have what you like."

"Do you enjoy tea, Frank?"

"As a matter of fact, I do," Frank grinned. "You want a cup?"

"Yes, please."

"All I have is black and some honey that I put in, is that okay?" Frank asked, walking toward his kitchenette.

"That is fine, thank you."

Frank went and set the water to boil and then, resting against the countertop, turned to look at Stan. "So, we haven't talked about the wound."

"We have not."

"Knife fight?" Frank asked.

Stan nodded. "Quite skilled, too. He simply lacked the anger to make his skill lethal this evening."

"I'm assuming you killed him, whoever he is," Frank continued. "You put the body somewhere, and I don't want to know where."

"That is good," Stan remarked. "I would not have told you anyway. The business is between myself and the man I am looking to kill."

"You sound like a friend of mine out in New Hampshire. Hell bent like you."

Stan frowned and tilted his head to one side like the old RCA mascot. "Who is this person? I may know them."

"Stranger things have happened," Frank said. "His name is Shane."

"Ah," Stan nodded. "Shane Ryan. Yes, I have met him. He is the one who put me in contact with Tom Daniels and assisted me with other tasks. Tom is an excellent young man."

"That he is," Frank agreed. "It's why I agreed to help you. Tom doesn't help random people. When he told me he would vouch for you, that was it. A done deal. He's got a lot of heart, and he's been through too much."

"He likes you."

Stan's statement caught Frank off-guard. "Well, yeah. I like him, too. I like to think that if I ever get around to having kids, then at least one of them is going to turn out like Tom Daniels. That's the hope. But I'm not looking to get married. I had a fiancé for a bit, but that ended a while back. Anyway, I'm kind of enjoying the whole single life. Sure, I go out and have fun, but I don't want to be married. Not anymore. That ship has passed, as the saying goes."

Stan nodded.

"Are you married?" Frank asked.

Stan shook his head. "There is a woman whose company I enjoy. I like her tremendously, if I am, to be honest. However, I do not believe she should be shackled with me."

"What if she doesn't think of a relationship with you as being shackled?" Frank asked.

"We will discuss it if the subject should come up," Stan answered after a moment. "She is a good person. I am fortunate that she enjoys my company."

"Make sure you hold onto it, then," Frank advised. "Anyway, we should be able to finish cleaning you up and getting you bandaged. You ready?"

"Of course," Stan told him.

Frank pulled on a fresh pair of gloves and went back to work.

Chapter 48
PANIC

A boom in the distance caused Ezra to tumble out of bed, the world a haze, then a shock as the motion sensor light came on. His heart raced, and no matter how hard he tried, he could not bring it back under control. His breath came in short, sharp inhalations, and when he got to his feet, his body trembled as though the entire building shook.

Before he could stop himself, Ezra reached out and slapped the panic button on his bedside table.

It took Robert less than thirty seconds to come through the bedroom door.

The man looked disheveled, his hair a mess and eyes puffy with sleep. He wore a pair of gray sweatpants and a matching tee shirt, items of clothing Ezra had never seen him in before.

"Are you okay, sir?" Robert asked, his voice raspy.

Ezra began to speak, then stopped. He managed to regain a semblance of control for a moment. "I do not feel safe here, Robert."

Robert straightened up. "What do you need me to do?"

"You know the storage locker on Webster Street?" Ezra asked.

"The one we rented after the move down here?"

"That's the one," Ezra nodded. "There is a .44 caliber handgun in the box marked Office I. The ammunition is in it. Could you bring the weapon and the ammunition here?"

"Yes, sir," Robert replied. "Where is the key?"

"In the office, placed in the file labeled Office I," Ezra told him.

"Do you want to come with me?" Robert asked. "To make sure you're safe?"

"While I do not feel safe here," Ezra began. "I am afraid my fear would be even worse should I step outside the building."

"I understand, sir," Robert said. "Please, stay here, in your room. I will double-check each level as I leave."

"Thank you, Robert," Ezra murmured.

Robert nodded and left the room, closing the door behind him.

Ezra hesitated only a moment before hurrying to the door and locking it. He didn't know if it would stop Stan Owens, but he hoped it would.

✳ ✳ ✳

Stan had declined painkillers from Frank, knowing full well that he needed absolute clarity. Ezra Pettigrew had sent an assassin to finish him off in the street, regardless of witnesses. This meant the man was desperate, and while desperate men made mistakes, there was always the possibility that their irrational gambles might pay off. The stitches in Stan's chest were a testament to that.

And just as he couldn't risk the painkillers slowing him down, neither could he sit in the motel room and recuperate.

Pettigrew's desperation had to be capitalized on. A mistake would be made.

And so, Stan sat in the darkness, the noise of the city a dull thrum in the small hours after midnight. He watched the front of Pettigrew's building, knowing the man had burrowed himself in and that if he were to do anything, need anything, it would be brought to him. So, Stan waited to see who would enter the building.

Surprise swept over him as he saw the front door open, and Pettigrew's man stepped out into the street. Stan watched the man pull a hood up over his head, slip his hands into the front pocket of the sweatshirt, and then hurry off to the left.

Stan kept pace, first at a safe distance, but when he realized that the man was not worried about being followed, Stan closed the distance.

The man was focused, glancing from side to side, not in a sense of worry, but as though he was searching for a street.

Ten minutes later, the man paused, then crossed the street and went down another.

And Stan followed.

In a short time, they came to a large, self-storage facility, and Stan waited well outside the gate as Pettigrew's man punched in a code and then entered the gated lot.

Robert's head ached as he went down the main aisle between the orange-door storage containers. As he approached the unit rented by Mr. Pettigrew, he passed one that was partially open. A dull light escaped from it, as did the sound of voices and the clink of a bottle. A moment later, a smell of body odor and bad whiskey reached him, and Robert nearly gagged. He had heard of people living in storage units, but he had always chalked it up to an urban myth.

He shook his head, able, unfortunately, to imagine what it might be like in that unit. He would need to speak about it to Mr. Pettigrew in the morning. It wouldn't do to have anything valuable near people living in a storage unit. He didn't care how elitist or unsympathetic that might sound, the fact remained there were important items stored in the unit until such time as Mr. Pettigrew decided what to do with them.

Robert reached the company's unit, unlocked the door and entered it. A motion-sensor light burst into life above him and illuminated the shelves lining the walls. Plastic boxes, each labeled in Abigail's neat, precise script, gave an accurate accounting of each box's contents.

Robert read the descriptions, moving from box to box and hoping the pistol wouldn't be in the last one opened.

It was not.

He found one labeled ".44 & Rounds." Robert took it down, opened it, and removed the pistol and the bullets. A quick glance at the other boxes helped him find a canvas tote bag, and so he put the weapon and the ammunition into it, covering them with a table runner Abigail had used to set out for Thanksgiving.

Robert stepped out, locked the door behind him, and started the walk back to the office.

✳ ✳ ✳

Stan had measured the distance from the office to the storage unit. It was less than a mile.

"Ray," he murmured.

The ghost appeared. "What's up?"

"Would you do me the kindness of staying here and keeping an eye on this facility?" Stan asked.

"This place?" Ray asked, nodding to the storage facility.

"Yes. Am I looking out for the guy you've been following?"

"That is correct," Stan replied.

"Sure, I can do that. What should I do if he shows back up? Should I come and find you?"

Stan shook his head. "No. If he returns, stay here and watch him, see what he does and where he goes."

"You got it," Ray grinned. "You going after him now?"

"I am," Stan confirmed, then set off to follow Pettigrew's man.

It took only a minute to find the man, who returned directly to Pettigrew's building. Stan watched the man enter, lock the door once again, and then disappear into the building's interior.

Staying in the shadows, Stan waited and considered what to do next.

CHAPTER 49
AN EASY JOB

"You need me to come in?" Alan asked, shifting the truck into park, the lights having been turned off several minutes prior.

Jerry shook his head and ejected the magazine of his Glock. "Nah. I'm good."

He slid the magazine back in, chambered a round and grinned at Alan. "Remember, it's just some lady in there. No real security, nothing to worry about. I'll go in, take care of her, then get the back open so we can load everything up."

Alan gave him a thumbs up. "Cool. I'll be right here."

Jerry nodded, climbed out of the truck and walked toward the small house with the attached barn that served as Morrigan's business. He glanced around, appreciating the isolation of the building. The house sat in the center of several cleared acres, and several more acres of woods surrounded that.

Perfect for an uninterrupted removal of a problem.

Jerry was only concerned about whether or not he had been given the right address. Pettigrew had been agitated, and it wouldn't be the first time someone who was upset gave him the wrong address.

And Jerry, unlike Paulo, did not shoot first and ask questions later. He avoided prison as much as possible, and gunning down the wrong person was never a good idea.

Still, he needed to get in, have a look around and see if he was in the right place.

He kept to the right of the house, following the wall and searching for a side or rear entrance. He had no desire to try the front door, and a quick walk around the perimeter would let him know if anyone was awake.

Jerry reached the connection between the house and the barn and stopped as a door on the connection swung open. A bright light blinded him, and he kept his gun arm down.

"Who are you?" a male voice asked from behind him, and Jerry swore. He started to turn, and the speaker snapped, "Don't move!"

Jerry stopped.

"I asked you a question," the man stated. "Who are you?"

"Name's Jerry," he replied. "I came to pick up some stuff for Mr. Pettigrew."

"There's nothing here for him," came the reply. "You should leave."

"Yeah, I should," Jerry nodded and spun halfway around, dropping to one knee and bringing his pistol up. He snapped off two shots at the man standing behind him, but both seemed to miss.

The man rushed toward him and Jerry steadied his hand, squeezing off two more shots which should have knocked the man backward.

Nothing happened.

A heartbeat later, the man was there. Jerry could see the night sky through the stranger, and then everything went dark.

Alan knew Jerry didn't like it when he drank on the job, but Alan didn't appreciate driving out to the middle of nowhere at the last minute, either. And besides, Jerry wouldn't find out. Alan had been chewing on mints the whole drive, and he was going to keep chewing on them after he had a couple of pulls off the bottle of Wild Irish Rose he had brought with him. He took the bottle out of the pocket behind his seat, uncapped it and then shuddered as a cold breeze snapped through the truck.

He turned to see if he had opened his window, and the door was torn open. The bottle tumbled from his hands, and he struck the ground hard enough to knock the breath out of his lungs.

As he struggled to breathe, someone jerked his arms behind his back, secured his wrists, and then started dragging him into the darkness.

✳ ✳ ✳

Jerry opened his eyes and knew he would be dead soon.

He couldn't see anything, and despite still being clothed, the air was terribly cold. It took him a moment to realize he was bound to a folding chair, the metal creaking and groaning as he moved. He heard someone breathing and knew it wasn't Alan. If it had been, Jerry would have smelled the mints the man had been chewing constantly since Worcester.

"So, what now?" Jerry asked, although he knew exactly what was going to happen next.

"Now?" a woman asked. "You're going to die."

Jerry swallowed hard. "Where's Alan?"

"Alan is your companion?" she asked.

"Yes."

"He's gone on to his just reward, as the saying goes," she answered.

"Did you kill him?" Jerry asked.

"Would it be easier for you to know that I didn't?"

Jerry laughed. "No."

"Good, because I did," she stated. "I killed him, and in a few minutes, when his blood is done draining from his corpse, I will kill you."

"What?" Jerry shook his head. "What do you mean, draining blood?"

"I have a knife," she told him, her voice coming closer. "It is older than this country, forged when Hadrian built his wall in Britain. It has been fed the blood of ten thousand men, and it will feed from you as well."

"Listen, lady," he hissed. "I don't know what you're babbling about, but if you're going to kill me, get it over with."

"That's just the thing," she whispered, her tone painfully sweet. "It doesn't just feed on your blood, it feeds on your soul. No matter what you believe, and even if you believe in nothingness, your soul will feed it, give the iron strength, and keep it powerful."

An old fear, one from his youth, crept up. Memories of church services, of prayers said by the side of his bed, the fear of his soul not going to Heaven. All of it raced back to the forefront of these thoughts, and the sudden terror that accompanied them caused him to lose control of his bladder, soiling himself.

"Now you understand," the woman said, and he felt the sharp prick of a blade against his chest. Slowly, she started cutting away his clothes, and Jerry began to scream.

CHAPTER 50
UNWANTED

Once Robert entered the office and set the pistol and ammunition on the table, Ezra opened his laptop, typed in several commands, and then listened.

Faint thumps could be heard, each one representing a small door opening and releasing a ghost into a secured area. Ezra had seen the footage of Owens dealing with the dead, but he hoped one of the ghosts might be able to do what couldn't be done so far. If not kill him, perhaps even dissuade him from continuing should the man breach the walls of the building.

The pistol was in case Owens reached Ezra's apartment.

"Did you see anything?" he asked.

Robert shook his head, stifled a yawn and then rubbed his eyes. "No. Although one of the units near yours is occupied by some homeless men."

Ezra nodded absently, murmuring, "A problem for another day."

"Of course, sir."

"But you didn't see anyone?" Ezra asked.

"No, sir. Nothing at all."

"Good." Ezra sighed. "I hope it stays that way. I would like to get a halfway decent night's sleep."

Robert nodded in agreement.

Ezra's phone rang and caused them both to start. Robert let out a sheepish laugh, and Ezra forced a smile as he picked it up. He looked at the number, saw it was the one Jerry had used, and he answered.

"Hello, Jerry," Ezra greeted. "Did you find it easily enough?"

"Ezra," Morrigan said, and he stiffened, the phone almost falling from fingers stiff with fear.

Ezra tried to speak, but his mouth failed to work.

"You sent two men to see me," she continued. "Do me the kindness of not refuting it."

"I won't," he managed to whisper.

"Good. Let me tell you what I have done with them so you might understand the significance of this situation." She paused, and when he made no reply, the woman continued, "Both men are dead. Neither died quickly. I have bled them out and will use that blood to safeguard my property. I have skinned them, and I will stretch and tan their skins for drum hides. I need you to understand that I and my entire section of the world, are now off-limits to you. Is this understood?"

"Yes," he managed to say.

"Good. Three is power, Ezra, and I will craft three drums from Jerry. He was armed, and so his skin will be useful. Do not make me come to you, Ezra Pettigrew," she warned. "It will not be a pleasant experience."

She ended the call before he could respond.

Ezra looked to Robert, opened his mouth to speak, and the alarm shrieked. With fumbling fingers, Ezra brought up the security feed just in time to see Stan Owens kick in the safety glass and stride in.

✳ ✳ ✳

Stan entered the lobby of the building and made his way to the stairs. He would not trust the elevator in this place, and he suspected Pettigrew would be on the top floor.

Throwing open the door to the stairwell, he was not surprised to see the ghost of a young man standing, grinning. Stan ignored him as the ghost rushed at him.

The quick impact of cold through his flesh sent a shudder along his spine, but he continued up to the second flight of stairs. When he passed onto the second landing, both the young man and a second, murkier-shaped ghost stood there, and they attacked in unison.

The blows hurt, but only for a moment.

The dead vanished, and Stan continued up the stairs.

* * *

"Where are they going?" Ezra demanded, hating the nervous pitch of his voice. "Why do they keep disappearing?"

"I don't know," Robert whispered, his eyes fixed on the screen.

"Every time they touch him, they're cast aside," Ezra hissed. "It's like they can't bear to be near him."

They watched Owens pass through more of the dead. Some tried to attack, but they vanished. The others fell back.

"Will this even work?" Ezra asked, motioning toward the .44. "Can bullets even stop him?"

"They have to," Robert answered, but Ezra heard the doubt in the man's response. Heard it and felt it. He didn't know what to make of Stan Owens, but he was growing more terrifying with every step he took toward the top floor.

Ezra looked at the gun again and shuddered.

"We have to leave," Ezra whispered. "But we're trapped."

"No, sir," Robert replied. "We're not. There's still the fire escape. We can use that to get away."

"Are you sure?"

"I am if we leave now, sir. We can go and hide in the storage unit. That way, he won't find us, not there," Robert's words rushed out of him. "If we stay much longer, though. I don't know if we'll get away."

Ezra didn't hesitate. "Let's go."

The two men got to their feet, and Ezra followed Robert to the fire escape. Once Robert had the window open, he led the way out and onto the fire escape.

"Don't look down, sir," Robert told him. "Focus on what you're holding onto. Your feet will find the rungs as you go."

Without a word, Ezra nodded and started down.

✳ ✳ ✳

By the third floor, the dead no longer approached him.

Stan climbed the stairs steadily, focused only on the top floor. He would find Pettigrew there and Pettigrew's man as well. It would not matter. It would not matter, even if they had weapons.

Stan would kill them both, even if it meant dying. He would regret not being with Gwen, but he would be dead, and there would be nothing for him to worry about.

On the fifth floor, Stan found himself standing in front of a closed door.

He reached for it, and a ghost appeared on his left.

Stan lowered his arm and turned to face the spirit of a woman in her early thirties. She did not look as though she bore him any ill will, but that could not be used as a measure of danger.

Plenty had looked upon him with kindness in the past, and then they had tried to kill him.

"The door is locked," she told him.

"Then it will be difficult to break down," he replied.

She inclined her head in agreement. "There is another way."

He waited.

"I can move the lock," she continued. "The tumblers are easy. Is this something you would like?"

"I would appreciate it," he replied cautiously.

She smiled an act which revealed shattered teeth. "I will help you."

"Thank you."

"You do not ask why?" Her eyebrow arched over her left eye.

"I assume you have a reason," Stan stated. "Either Pettigrew or his man have done you wrong."

"His name is Robert, and he has done nothing wrong. At least not to us. No, Pettigrew is the culprit, and if you can injure him, then we will also be happy. He has trapped us here with lead and salt and iron."

"I am sorry."

"Hurt him," she replied, her voice suddenly harsh. "Hurt him and make him pay for what he has done."

Stan nodded, and the woman disappeared.

A heartbeat later, the locks clicked in the door, and it swung open. He put his hand on the cold metal, shoved it aside, and approached the only door in the hallway in front of him.

He took hold of the knob and found it was locked. Before the ghosts could lend assistance again, Stan kicked it in. Splinters of wood exploded out into the room, and the door squealed as it was torn off its hinges. For a moment, it teetered, then crashed to the floor.

A window across the room allowed a cool breeze to blow through, and when he walked to it, he knew Pettigrew and Robert were gone. They had taken the fire escape to freedom.

But Stan would find them. He would find Ezra Pettigrew and punish him, and Robert, if that was necessary, too.

Stan stepped out onto the fire escape and looked around, searching for something familiar.

And then, he saw it. The storage units with their orange doors. He let his eyes roam over the streets, seeking out the straightest route and then seeing a pair of figures hurrying along the sidewalk, clinging badly to the shadows.

Two men moving toward the storage facility.

Ezra Pettigrew and his companion.

Stan went back into the room, walked past a desk and saw ammunition on the table. He hesitated, his fingers longing to grasp the cool brass, but he stopped himself.

Pettigrew was armed, but it would not make any difference.

Stan would kill Pettigrew with just his hands. If he couldn't, then it wasn't the man's time to die.

But Stan would do his best to make certain it was.

Chapter 51
At the Storage Facility

"We're here, sir," Robert said, his words rushed.

Ezra could only nod. He was in worse shape than he had thought, and he did not trust himself to speak without gasping. He watched as Robert punched in the code, and then they hurried along the main road into the facility.

Robert led the way easily, and in a short time, they were standing beside a storage unit that looked like every other. Ezra stood by as Robert unlocked the door, pulled it up and motioned for Ezra to go inside.

Lights came on as Robert stepped in and closed the door halfway, allowing for fresh air to circulate through the room.

"Owens doesn't know of this place?" Ezra asked.

Robert shook his head. "No. I've reviewed the footage from the previous few days, and there's nothing there."

"Were you able to review today's?" Ezra asked.

"No, but as soon as we have a laptop set up in here, I will check it."

Ezra nodded wearily and sat down on the floor.

Robert paused, then went about finding a laptop in the various supplies. He needed to make sure the facility was secure.

"Did they go in?" Stan asked.

"Yeah," Ray nodded. "Not too far. You'll see them, they ducked into one of the storage units. They left it open, too."

"Thank you, Ray," Stan said. "Did you happen to see the code they used to get in?"

The dead man's shoulders sagged. "No. I didn't even think about it."

"That is fine, Ray. I will find another way in. They will not be difficult to locate, not if they are the only ones with the door open. I know them both," Stan explained. "I will see their faces. Please keep an eye on this entrance while I look for an alternate way into the lot."

"Okay."

Stan left the dead man near the entrance and started on the left, following the fence and peering in as he went. He didn't see any cars or trucks, no motorcycles or mopeds, nothing that would hint at someone other than Pettigrew and Robert being inside. It would make the killing easier, knowing he would not have to worry about any others. There would be no chance for unwanted casualties.

✳ ✳ ✳

As Robert sought to establish a secure connection and gain access to the surveillance system, Ezra got to his feet.

Robert glanced up from the work, frowning. "Sir, shouldn't you be sitting down?"

"No, but thank you for your concern," Ezra replied. He looked at the .44 caliber pistol in his hand. He turned the cylinder and said, "I'm going to take a look outside."

Robert's eyes widened, and Ezra let out a tired laugh.

"I am not going on patrol, Robert," Ezra assured him. "My plan is to stay near the unit and keep an eye out. I am most certainly not wandering around."

Robert hesitated, then nodded. "I worry, sir."

"And I am alive because of your worry, and Abigail's as well," Ezra reminded him. "I trust you both. Now, please trust me to do this. And, quite frankly, I have to. If I sit and do nothing, I will fall apart."

"I understand, sir."

Ezra stepped under the door and out into the cool night air. Off to one side, he heard a pair of muted voices and realized they were coming from another storage unit. For a moment, he tightened his grip on the pistol, and then he relaxed, remembering what Robert had told him, how some men were living in one of the units.

Ezra turned his attention away from them and focused once more on the facility as a whole and the perimeter fence in particular.

Stan continued his examination of the fence, pausing as a pick-up truck hauling a trailer of battered lawnmowers and leaf blowers pulled up to an apartment building across the street. He stayed hidden as a man and woman exited the truck, both obviously drunk as they staggered toward the front stairs. In a few moments, the couple entered the building, and Stan was on the move again.

He rounded the corner, the apartment building behind him and the storage facility on his right, glancing back and forth as he went.

And then he saw it. A mass of pallets stacked against the fence, an easy climb to the top and a soft drop to the bottom. His stitches might tear, but it was easier to go to the emergency room to have stitches replaced than it was to go and have them done in the first place.

Stan walked to the pallets and began to climb.

The clatter of wood caught Ezra's attention, and he stepped over to peer around one of the storage units. He stiffened as he caught sight of Stan Owens climbing up a pile of pallets toward the top of the facility's fence.

Fear gripped him as he raised the pistol up, the weapon trembling in his hand as he brought it to bear on Owens. He tried to steady it with his free hand, but even then, the weapon shook, and with every heartbeat, the man moved closer to the top.

Ezra squeezed the trigger and then gasped in surprise as the pistol fired, bucking in his hands and sending Stan Owens tumbling down.

For a moment, Ezra stood where he was, still pointing the weapon toward the pile of pallets. When no noise or movement issued forth, he turned and ran for Robert.

When he ducked under the half-open door, Ezra found Robert standing up, a look of concern and fear on his face.

"Are you alright, sir?"

Ezra nodded, looked at the pistol and tossed it to one side. "I think I just killed Owens."

"How?"

"He was climbing pallets to get in, and I shot him," Ezra answered. "I saw him go down, and he didn't get back up."

Robert looked around, confused, and then a look of determination came over him. "We can't take the chance that he is still alive."

"But I shot him," Ezra began.

"I know, sir. But if you didn't kill him, we need to move. Now. Lock the facility, get to the airport, and fly out to meet Abigail."

Ezra wanted to argue, but as the adrenaline rush faded, he realized how right Robert was.

"Of course," Ezra nodded. "Let's go. We'll leave, as you said. I can charter a jet when we get to the airport."

With a sense of relief, Ezra rubbed his face with both hands and found himself looking forward to the unscheduled flight.

✴ ✴ ✴

"You're not dead."

Stan opened his eyes and looked up. Ray leaned over him, the night sky barely visible through the dead man's translucence and the streetlights.

"No," Stan agreed, still lying on his back, his head aching. "I most certainly am not. How long have I lain here, not dead?"

"Maybe ten minutes. I don't know, time's iffy for me. I went back and checked on them a few minutes ago. I saw the door open just a hair and could hear someone talking."

Stan sat up and groaned. The ache in his head morphed into a throb, and when he reached up and touched it, he winced. His fingers came away slick with blood. He probed the wound with his fingers and found it was nothing more than a shallow groove above his right ear.

"Do you know what happened?" Stan asked.

"You were shot."

Stan frowned, and anger built within him. "I was shot."

Ray nodded.

"Shot."

The anger shifted to rage, and Stan found himself getting to his feet. Ray spoke, but the words were unintelligible. A small, weak part of Stan struggled to regain control, but there was nothing it could do.

The rage took over.

Stan walked to the trailer parked in front of the apartment building and found a gas container and motor oil tucked away between some shovels. Walking up to the truck, he discovered the door was unlocked, and a quick search of the interior provided a working lighter and a battered and torn tee shirt.

The world became silent as he squatted down and added some of the oil to the gasoline and then tore the tee shirt into strips, feeding the longer ones into the plastic gas container. He watched, his heart thudding in his wound and his forehead, as the fabric absorbed the mixture. When it was ready, Stan stood and carried it back to the storage facility. He climbed up the pallets until he stood at the same height as the wall. He glanced around and saw Ray.

"Show me," Stan commanded, and the ghost entered the fenced-in area. He came to a stop in front of a unit a short distance away.

In the glare of the safety lights, each flickering with Ray's presence, Stan could make out a single unit with its door open a few inches. Ray hesitated, then pointed at the door.

The distance was not far.

The container of gas and oil was lighter than it looked.

Stan brought out the stolen lighter, lit the rag and held the container to make sure the fabric was well on its way to burning

Then he threw it.

The red plastic container arced, tumbling end over end to crash a few feet from the door. The plastic cracked, oil and gas spilling out as the container slid to a stop against the door. Flames jumped from the burning rag to the leaking fluids, and a moment later, liquid fire raced under the door.

Screams pierced the night, reverberating off the metal door and breaking through the silence Stan's rage had induced.

He stood a moment longer, looking at the inferno and listening to Pettigrew and Robert burn alive. The rage in him mirrored the flames, and he forced it back as best he could.

When he had gotten enough control over his anger, he turned around, climbed down the pallets, and walked back to his motel room.

CHAPTER 52

A HARD TRUTH

"He's not dead."

Morrigan sighed. "I thought it was too good to be true."

Lisbeth nodded and took a sip of her coffee, then continued, "Yeah. The two dead men were homeless. They managed to break into the storage unit next to Pettigrew's, which is how the mistake was made. Whoever was trying to kill Pettigrew evidently thought he was hiding in that one."

"But he wasn't."

Lisbeth shook her head. "Nope. I managed to recover some of the CCTV footage from different places, and you can track Pettigrew going to and coming back from the facility."

"Did you manage to find out where he went afterward?" Morrigan asked.

"Yeah. He went to the airport, chartered a private jet and took off."

"Do we know where?"

"I'm still hunting that information down," Lisbeth replied. "Are you going after him?"

"No. Well, at least not yet," Morrigan answered. "I may have to at some point, especially after he sent those two idiots out here to kill me and take our stock. But for now, I just want to know where he is."

"He looked like he was in rough shape," Lisbeth added. "Compared to other images and footage of him I've seen. I don't know if he'll be at the top of his game any time soon."

"I doubt he will ever be that confident," Morrigan agreed. "Whoever was trying to kill him came quite close."

"I have footage of that gentleman," Lisbeth told her. "If you want to look him up, too."

Morrigan shook her head. "No need. Unless he discovers that Pettigrew is still alive, I doubt the man will be of any use. Whoever he is should be alone with his peace."

Lisbeth raised an eyebrow. "Where's my bloodthirsty sister?"

Morrigan grinned. "Still here, just being a little more practical now. Some men earn their peace, just as some earn their death."

Lisbeth chuckled, finished her coffee and stretched in her chair.

"Going to get some sleep?" Morrigan asked.

"In a few minutes," her sister answered. "I need to make a quick call."

"To Tom?"

Lisbeth blushed. "Yes, to Tom. He's great, Morrigan. There's no pressure from him. Not like some of the others I've dated. He trusts me."

"That's important," Morrigan replied. "Trust is huge. I'm glad he trusts you. And do you trust him?"

"I do," Lisbeth nodded. "Weird, but yeah, I trust him. I'm thinking of moving in with him."

Morrigan blinked, surprised. "Really?"

"Not right away," Lisbeth laughed. "Not by a long shot. But I'm definitely thinking about it. I asked Tom about decorating some parts of his house, and he told me to do whatever made me happy."

It was Morrigan's turn to laugh. "Wow. I remember the fights Mom and Dad would have over the littlest things."

"Me, too," Lisbeth agreed. "I think that's what made his offer so surprising."

"Well, I'm going to be the big sister here and remind you not to jump right into this."

Lisbeth grinned. "Don't worry about that. I won't."

They stood up from the table and walked toward the kitchen.

"What about you?" Lisbeth asked when they set the mugs down in the sink.

"What about me?"

"You look happy, which is kind of an odd thing for you," Lisbeth remarked.

"True. Well, I have an old friend coming over. We'll catch up about old times, people we knew. All the usual stuff," Morrigan explained.

"Huh. For a minute, I thought you might have a boyfriend."

Morrigan folded her arms over her chest and raised one eyebrow.

"Fine!" Lisbeth laughed. "The ice queen doesn't need a boyfriend. Oh, wait, I said that wrong. She doesn't want a boyfriend."

Morrigan grinned. "Come on, I'll walk you to your car."

They exited the house and followed the long path to where Lisbeth's car was parked and where the U-Haul had been only a day before. It, like the two men who had come to kill Morrigan, now lay beneath the water of an old granite quarry on her land.

Life, as far as Morrigan was concerned, was good.

CHAPTER 53

HOME

Gwen sat him down at the table and shook her head. Her smile was one of love and concern.

"You should go to an emergency room," she told him, stepping over to the sink.

"They would question me," Stan replied.

"I'm going to question you."

"And I love you," he told her. "I trust you."

She glanced over her shoulder at him, a shy smile on her face. In a soft voice, she said, "I love you, too."

He watched as she filled the teapot with hot water and then set it to boil on the stove. When she finished, she retrieved a first aid kit from under the sink and brought it to the table.

"Now that you're done," she began, "do you think you can tell me what you were doing?"

"Yes," he answered. He closed his eyes and let her turn his head so she could look at the wound. "I was hunting down the man responsible for Adam's death."

"Did you find him?"

"I did."

"Is everything, well, taken care of?"

"It is."

"Do you want to tell me about it?" She took out alcohol and cotton swabs from her first aid kit.

"If I tell you, it might put you in danger, should it ever come back to me," Stan whispered. "I was unkind, and I let my temper get the better of me."

She turned his head and kissed him lightly on the lips. "If it comes back, I'll stand beside you, Stan Owens. Someone hurt your friend. You went and hurt them back, didn't you?"

He could only nod in reply.

"Then tell me what you did," she said, her voice strong. "I can only love you more. Never less."

As she started cleaning his wound, Stan told her what he had done, when he had done it, and to whom he had done it.

Gwen rocked back and forth in her chair, a small, knitted blanket over her lap. The squeak of the wood runners against the floor soothed her, her rocking in perfect unison with the light, easy breathing of Stan as he slept.

She had bundled him up in her bed, piled pillows high around him and made certain his head was elevated. She was worried about the gouge left in his skin and the stitches from the knife wound. She had cleaned both, replaced two of the stitches with her own, and then stitched up the gouge. That should have been treated much earlier, but he had been right about it bringing too much attention in a hospital setting. Professionals were trained to look for wounds like that, and even if the patient didn't want to report an assault, the police would be notified.

There was always the chance that the person in the ER wasn't the victim of a crime. Occasionally, they were the perpetrator.

And this had been the case with Stan.

By his own account, he had left a trail of bodies behind him. The last two would be considered the worst.

A pair of men burned alive in a storage facility in Worcester, Massachusetts.

And Gwen was worried. Not of him, but for him. She did not want the police to come looking for him.

She would, she decided as she looked at him, lie. She would tell them he was with her, staying here and recuperating emotionally and mentally from the death of not one but two friends.

Gwen would protect him, no matter what.

"Are you all right?"

His question took her by surprise, and she looked at him, smiling. He had turned his head and faced her without her senses registering even the slightest of movements.

"Yes," she answered. "I'm fine. I just didn't want to disturb you."

"Disturb me?" He sat up in the bed and moved over. "I am in your bed, and you are caring for me. How can you disturb me? I am disturbing you."

She got up, folded the blanket and set it on the rocker before going to the bed. She climbed in and kissed him.

"You will never disturb me, Stan. You make me happy, and it takes a lot for me to be truly happy." She traced the line of his jaw with her finger. "I can't tell you the last time I felt this good. This is what I want. To be here, with you, in this house, and nothing more."

He reached up with both hands and gently touched her face and hair. In a voice raw with emotion, he whispered, "I cannot remember the last time I was happy, Gwen. I cannot remember the last time I wanted to be with someone, to hear their voice, to smell them with every breath. You are perfection. I cannot understand this, nor will I attempt to. I accept it as the gift I know it to be."

Stan pulled her in close, and they sank down onto the bed together. She brought the blanket up around their shoulders and embraced him.

In the stillness of the house, she closed her eyes, rested her head upon his chest and listened to the slow, steady beating of his heart.

Check out these best-selling series from our talented authors:

GHOST STORIES

RON RIPLEY
BERKLEY STREET SERIES
MOVING IN SERIES
HAUNTED COLLECTION SERIES
DEATH HUNTER SERIES

IAN FORTEY
JIGSAW OF SOULS SERIES
CULT OF THE ENDLESS NIGHT SERIES

SUPERNATURAL SUSPENSE

A. I. NASSER
SLAUGHTER SERIES
SIN SERIES

DAVID LONGHORN
NIGHTMARE SERIES
ASYLUM SERIES

SARA CLANCY
THE BELL WITCH SERIES
BANSHEE SERIES

For a complete list of our new releases and best-selling horror books, visit
ScareStreet.com or scan the QR code below!

www.ingramcontent.com/pod-product-compliance
Lightning Source LLC
Chambersburg PA
CBHW050341030726
47503CB00008B/2550